Critical Acclaim for Shena Mackay

'In *Music Upstairs* she tells the breathless tale of Sidonie, a typist who gets cheesed off with things and drifts zombie-like through an affair first with her landlord's wife and then with the landlord, a pair of voguey-poguey layabouts. It is scruffy, sweaty, shapeless, desultory, vivid and heavy with inchoate poetry of adolescence: a right rave along the Earls Court Road and boozers adjacent' – *Daily Telegraph*

'*Music Upstairs* may earn all sorts of literary comparisons, but the most obvious influences are Godard and Truffaut. Shena Mackay's narrative has a marvellous unblinking clarity . . . *Music Upstairs* is as individual as it is contemporary'
– *Sunday Times*

'Mackay [writes] with exuberant glee and compassionate horror about people living in surburban sorriness and desolation' – *Times Literary Supplement*

'A rococo writer, noticing people and things with both murderous innocence and fantastical ingenuity . . . she captures moods and moments with a sly accuracy' – *Observer*

'Here is a woman who can write nearly everyone else off their feet' – *Financial Times*

'The supreme lyricist of daily grot is still Shena Mackay'
– *New Statesman*

'She stands on her own – an original and a very hot property'
– *Daily Mail*

SHENA MACKAY

was born in Edinburgh in 1944 and educated at Tonbridge
Girls' Grammar School and Kidbrooke Comprehensive
School. She left at the age of sixteen and has worked at a
variety of jobs – as an artist's model, a library assistant, for a
herbalist, and in a greetings card factory and an antique shop.

Written at the age of seventeen, Shena Mackay's first novel,
Dust Falls on Eugene Schlumburger/Toddler on the Run (1964),
was published to critical acclaim. *Music Upstairs* appeared a
year later and was followed by *Old Crow* (1967); *An Advent
Calendar* (1971); *A Bowl of Cherries* (1984) and *Redhill Rococo*,
which was published in 1986 and awarded the Fawcett
Society Prize a year later. Her seventh novel, *Dunedin*, will
appear in 1990. She has also published two collections of short
stories, *Babies in Rhinestone* (1983) and *Dreams of Dead
Women's Handbags* (1987). Some of her short stories have been
broadcast and they have also been published in a variety of
magazines.

Shena Mackay is a regular reviewer for the *Sunday Times*.
She has received an Arts Council Bursary and a Society of
Authors Travelling Scholarship and has taught on creative
writing courses. She has three grown-up daughters and lives
in London, where she is a member of the Green Party and
various environmental and Animal Rights and Welfare orga-
nizations.

VIRAGO
MODERN
CLASSIC

NUMBER

318

SHENA MACKAY

Music Upstairs

VIRAGO

Published by VIRAGO PRESS Limited 1989
20-23 Mandela Street, Camden Town, London NW1 OHQ

First published in Great Britain by Andre Deutsch Limited 1965
Copyright © Shena Mackay 1965
Afterword Copyright © Shena Mackay 1989

A CIP record for this book is available from the British Library

Printed in Great Britain by Cox & Wyman Ltd., Reading, Berks

'When I grow Too Old to Dream'
Lyric by Oscar Hammerstein II, Music by Sigmund Romberg.
© Copyright 1934–1935 Metro-Goldwyn-Mayer Inc., New York.
Rights throughout the world controlled by
Robbins Music Corporation, New York.
Robbins Music Corporation Ltd., London.
J. Albert & Sons Pty Ltd., Sydney, Australia.
Used by permission.

Lyric page 39 from 'White Christmas'
Copyright © 1942 Irving Berlin.
Words included by permission of Irving Berlin Limited,
14 St George Street, Hanover Square, London W1.

We have been unable to trace the copyright holder for the painting, 'Julia and
Starky' by Anna Zinkeisen, reproduced on the cover and would be grateful
for any information.

In a summer of sudden storms, the day after moving with her friend Joyce to a new address in Earls Court, Sidonie took the Southern Railway to Penge. When she returned in the purple evening, her unexplained fear grew as she neared the intercom. She stepped backwards into the road and looked up; behind the closed red curtains the light burned, but, unable to shout, she had to climb the steps and press the bell, clearing her throat and rehearsing what to say in the short silence that rang in her ears.

'Who is it?'

'Sidonie.'

'Who?'

'Sidonie O'Neill.'

A buzzer sounded and she tried to push the door, but nothing happened. She pressed the bell again and Mrs Beacon's voice floated through the grille:

'Take the handle in your hand and when the buzzer sounds, pull it towards you and push.'

The door opened and she ran upstairs in relief and humiliation, past the Beacons' door, dreading to meet one of them.

Joyce was sitting on her bed, applying reptile polish to a pair of crocodile shoes. A bunch of blue cornflowers stood in a milk bottle in front of the mirror, and the sounds of the hot night, laughter and cars, came through the open window.

'Have a nice time?'

'All right. Anything exciting happened?'

'No. Oh yes. I had dinner with them,' indicating the kitchen with a shoe whose scales were dull with polish.

'They're ever so nice, Sidonie, you'd like them. They're called Pam and Lenny.'

'Do they like each other?'

'Oh yes, they seem to. Lenny said she was one of the best cooks he knew and she said Thank you darling.'

'One of. What did you have?'

'Oh, soup and lamb and potatoes and beans.'

'Runner?'

'Baked.'

Sidonie, with the memory of a pale little heap of scrambled egg on the vast white plate – her mother had been out, and the bent coin stuck in a chocolate machine – conceded that she might like the Beacons.

'What does he do?'

'Salesman. Pam thinks he talks like a BBC announcer. Have you noticed he sometimes leaves the g's off the ends of his words?'

'No. I've hardly spoken to him. Come out with us to get something to eat?'

'Didn't you have anything at your Mum's?'

'Of course, but I'm still starving. Come on, Joyce.'

'No. I've got to do these shoes for work.'

'I'll do them for you when we get back.'

Joyce put down her duster and stood up, pushing her feet into flat shoes and pulling her skirt round.

'Oh come on,' said Sidonie as she stood in front of the mirror, a comb in her hair and mascara in her hand. Sidonie did not know why she had to hurry past Beacons', but in doing so slipped, her shoe flew off and she sat down on the stairs and was sitting when the door opened and Lenny Beacon, in cotton shorts and with a smear of lipstick above his lip, appeared.

'Where are you off to at this late hour?'

'We're going to get something to eat,' said Joyce, smiling and pulling at Sidonie's arm, drowning her 'It's not late'.

'If you're hungry, help yourself from our larder. Any time.'

'It's all right, really, we want to go out,' said Sidonie, but 'Oh thanks, Mr Beacon' and Joyce was already three stairs up.

'I told you to call me Lenny and that goes for you too.'

Sidonie smiled before turning and walking upstairs with Lenny Beacon's eyes on her back and his bare feet following.

A patch of sweat collected under Lenny's toes as he stood in front of the cupboard, surveying, then was spread as he carried a loaf on a bread-board and set it down among the blue formica roses on the table. Sidonie looked out of the window on to the station, where the hot asphalt shimmered under lights, and Joyce spread circles of bread with butter and apricot jam.

'Couldn't you do something constructive, like find two plates for instance?'

'Don't let's bother with plates.'

'Lazy little bugger, isn't she?' said Lenny and she knew it was a compliment.

Later, the door opened and Sidonie, the brush in her hair and her face above refracted cornflowers in the triple glass, turned and the face of Lenny Beacon came round the door. Joyce turned in bed, the cigarette poised between mouth and ashtray, and pulled the sheet up over the torn nightdress.

'Sorry to disturb you, girls. I've brought the rent book. Have either of you a pen? – I'll just fill in this week.' His eyes were on a red bra on the floor.

'I'm afraid there's only this eyebrow pencil.'

'Fine.'

And as if eyebrow pencil was the medium with which he always filled in rent books at 1.10 Lenny Beacon put the book on the mantelpiece and pressing hard, forced the blunt point to inscribe in looped writing their names and the date and the amount paid.

'I'll leave it on the mantelpiece, shall I?'

'Yes, thanks.'

He walked towards the door.

'I'll wish you ladies good night then,' picking up the red bra and putting it on a chair.

'Haven't you anything better to put those flowers in? I'll see if Pam's got a vase in the kitchen.'

'Oh yes – we've got plenty of vases. Milk bottles are the latest thing, didn't you know?'

'Really? Is that what they're using now? Oh – I see. Good night, then.'

He closed the door quietly and they heard the kitchen

door open and the sound of a toothbrush against a mug
and running water.

'So what's wrong with borrowing a vase? Better than
that milk bottle anyway.'

'We don't want to keep accepting things from them.
I mean, you can eat their food, but I'm not going to. I
think he's sort of sinister. Anyway, she'll only hate us if
he's too friendly with us.'

'I suppose you think he fancies you.'

'Yes.'

Sidonie put out the light and lay in bed under the hot
blankets, her head resting on the cool wallpaper above
her head.

'Do you fancy him?'

'Give me credit for a little taste.'

Joyce's voice, growing fainter from the opposite bed,
among creaking springs, said, 'No more Room 5, five
rings, Sid, isn't it wonderful?'

'Yes, I suppose so; but maybe it's better not to be the
only tenants.'

'No! Anyway, there's people in the basement.'

A bottle smashed in the street below and music came
up from Beacons.

'Joyce! Joyce!'

The alarm ringing and the sun beating through the red curtains woke Sidonie to the sound of children shouting behind the thin wall and a baby crying.

'Joyce! Get up, the alarm's gone.'

Joyce lay on her back in her blue nightdress in disarray of sheets, a faint line of sweat above her upper lip and along the creases of her eyelids in the traces of blue eyeshadow. Sidonie shook her till she woke and made her wash first. Joyce got up sighing from the bed and went out to the bathroom.

As they walked along the road, early for work, Sidonie thought she discerned L. Beacon's head at a third-floor window, but couldn't be sure if it was the correct house. Nausea like an escalator travelled up and down her as she travelled to work and as she took the green cover from the typewriter, water-proofed although the rains of Holborn could not penetrate those steel walls, she had to rest her head for a moment on the cool keys. Fran Marsh, the headphones already over her parallel ears, the clock showing 8.45 and her legs scarcely touching the floor, started on her third letter.

'Hi, Fran.'

There was no reply, and she remembered she was not being spoken to, on account of some hair lacquer. She went over to the window and lit a cigarette – girls in summer dresses were arriving at the plate-glass doors and laughing and joking as the sun grew hotter and streamed through the open slats of white Venetian blinds. This was a new experience for Sidonie: she had never arrived before nine-five and was greeted with 'Good afternoon' by the head of the typing pool – in the afternoon it was good evening.

'Coming swimming lunch time, Sidonie?'

'No, I can't, I've got to meet someone.'

The firm had its own swimming pool, table-tennis, hairdressing salon and dance hall, so that employees need not leave the premises until midnight. In the rail strike Fran Marsh, among others, had spent four days and nights in the building, to return fresh as a daisy to the bosom of her family to find no wardrobe; her clothes had been removed.

'Can't you see they only do it so we keep healthy and do more work?' said Sidonie.

'Some people are never grateful,' said the head of the dictaphone department.

'Grateful! They should be grateful to us.'

'We can easily get someone to fill your place.'

'Impossible.'

The clock above the filing cabinet said one o'clock, and Sidonie placing a wire tray over a wet patch where a man from Accounts had rested his hand, got up, laddering her stocking on the desk.

'Language,' said Fran, on her way to the lounge with a polythene bag of banana sandwiches.

Sidonie took off her stockings in the washroom and splashed water on her face. The rollermatic towel had stuck and a few soiled inches hung down, so she dried her face on her handkerchief and went down in the lift and took the underground to Green Park.

Lewis, with a bag of cherries, was waiting by the iron gate.

'You're late.'

'Sorry.'

'What happened on Friday?'

'I'm sorry, Lewis, really I am.'

'What happened?'

'I just felt too depressed and there was no way to contact you.'

'You could have rung me at the office, couldn't you?'

'I couldn't face explaining to you, and the switchboard asks you your name.'

'Don't you know it then? God! Shows how much you love me, if you can't even do that for me.'

'I said I'm sorry.'

'It isn't the first time either. There's someone else, isn't there?'

'No.'

'I suppose waiting for two and a half hours for someone isn't depressing, is it?'

'I don't know.'

The cherries he had bought became ludicrous and he kicked the bag so that they scattered on the grass.

'You think you can get away with anything, don't you?'

'Yes.'

'Right. That's it. I'm not the bloody office tea-boy, who you can twist round your little finger. You can phone me and apologize tomorrow if you like, and I'll consider accepting it. Good-bye.'

'We have tea-ladies,' she shouted after him, but he did not turn round and she did not go back to work.

When she met Pam Beacon for the first time that evening, hard golden body and brown hair hanging to her shoulders, she said afterwards to Joyce, 'She'd be all right if she shut up about children for five minutes,' and resumed brushing the black hair that fell either side of a white face.

Two days later, about 6.30 in the evening, Sidonie went into the kitchen to look for a tin-opener. Pam Beacon was changing the baby. A disposable nappy steamed on the floor beside her chair and a cigarette burned in the ashtray, among jars of cream and soap and baby powder. She fastened the pale pink paddi garment and bounced the baby in her arms, kissing all over its face as she caught it, her mouth wide open like a witch's.

'Oh look, I've got lipstick on the baby's hair, bless her.' The room smelled of zinc-and-castor-oil ointment and distemper. Lenny was distempering a wall and pale pink stars had solidified on his head and hands. Sidonie walked across to the draining board, suddenly clumsy with his eyes on her, her stiff legs shuffling on the linoleum. A knife crashed into the sink; the tin-opener wasn't there. She couldn't walk back across the vast kitchen so she leaned against the table and touched the baby's face with her finger; it was cold and thick like the skin of a three-day-old dead plaice she had once touched and her finger stuck slightly in a dent. The plaice had lain brown and blue and orange on a plate in the kitchen for five days and then was given to the dog who ate its skin as well.

Lenny held out the wiped brush to her and said:
'Like to do a bit?'

She took the brush, which seemed very heavy, and dipped it into the tin. Pink distemper ran down the handle and Lenny put his hand over hers and scraped the bristles against the rim of the tin and she placed the brush against the wall.

'Here, let me show you. Do it like this, see?'

'Yes.'

She applied another disjointed pink streak to the wall and tried to obliterate the tracks made by individual bristles.

'You put too much distemper on your brush. Here, let me show you. Get it?'

She started giggling, holding the brush as if her hand was joined on backwards at the wrist. Her face was burning and her hand collapsing.

'Talk about awkward,' said Pam.

She was conscious of her back and the backs of her legs facing Pam and the skin of her face and arms near Lenny's face. Each time paint splashed or dripped he took the brush and corrected her. Then Joyce came in – 'Where's that tin-opener then?' and she was able to sidle out with the walk which was to become permanent and a subject of the Beacons' mimicry.

The following evening Joyce went out straight from work and Sidonie wandered downstairs. The sitting-room door was open. She went on to the balcony where Pam stood with her arms resting on the railings, the white dress slipping off her shoulders and the smell of gardenias in the violet sky. As always with the first sips of Scotch, his face came back and she had to tell herself, don't think about Penge. She knocked back the drink and went inside and took a swig from the bottle and then another and refilled her tumbler and went back on to the balcony, and saw Pam smiling at her in a mist. Above the sound of traffic, the scent of gardenias drifted with smoke through her fingers as she threw her cigarette into the street and watched the red butt dying, then mangled by a car. She turned, a trace of ash on the white dress, and stretched out her hand, the wedding ring, the little emerald, clinked against Sidonie's glass and she took it, her lower lip reflected in the gold and returned it with a red smear below the rim.

'What are you thinking about?'

'Oh – nothing.'

'Lewis?'

'No.'

'I saw a gorgeous man in the supermarket today. Indian, I think, with the longest eyelashes you ever saw.'

'Oh – men. I've finished with them. I think I'll change to girls.'

'Do you? Really?'

'Yeah.' She snapped her cigarette in two and ground it against the railings. 'Yeah. I'm going down the Consul Club, see if I meet someone nice.' She was not.

'You'd soon get picked up if you went down there. I'd pick you up if I saw you down there.'

Sidonie turned and looked with a shock into the brown eyes very near her face.

'Would you?'

'Yes.'

Pam's face and smile blurred red and white and pink in front of her eyes. The glass clinked on her teeth.

'What would you say?'

'I'd buy you a drink.'

'Oh well, you can buy me one right now – or I'll get it. Can I get you one?'

'Thanks, love.'

Sidonie took both glasses and stumbling a little over the step through the French windows, walked over to the bar and put them down; her heart was thumping and a smile she couldn't take off kept coming to her lips. The bottle shook in her hand and hit the rim of the glass, pushing it so that the Scotch dripped on to the bar. She pushed it over the edge of the bar and into the lipstick-and-finger-smeared glass and refilled her own.

Pam took her glass and said, 'Don't look at me like that, love, I might rape you.'

Time passed, the traffic grew less, and there was Lenny pushing through the curtains with the nine-tenths-empty bottle.

'You greedy sows didn't leave me much, did you?' His head face voice and trousers an intrusion in the white evening. He raised the bottle to his mouth, his lips making a thick wet O round the rim, and wiped them on the back of his hand.

'What are you two looking so secretive about?'

'Secrets.'

'Don't be mean. Go on, tell me.'

'No.'

Lenny took out a packet of cigarettes and, not offering them, placed one in his mouth, lit it and took a long drag, exhaling grey smoke hard to show he needed it.

After a few minutes Pam put her arm round Lenny's shoulder where, after a slight shrug, it was allowed to remain, and they stood watching the moon rise over Earls Court.

The next day Sidonie came in at three in the hot afternoon and found Pam alone in the kitchen, looking out of the window over the shimmering tracks of the railway. A bucket of nappies boiled on the stove and a pool of water and disappearing bubbles lay under the legs of the washing machine.

'Hi. I'm just going to make a cup of coffee. Would you like one?' She said 'yes', although she wouldn't, and they sat opposite each other across the table. Words fell on the thick air as on the Dead Sea and Sidonie, not knowing what to do with her hands when the cup was empty, pushed a child's truck across the blue formica roses. It went too far and Pam picked it up and pushed it back, and they sat pushing the truck across the table until a child came in breaking the silence and taking the truck.

In the evening Joyce and Sidonie went to the Wayang with some friends.

'Old Dave's paying, aren't you, Dave? That's very nice of you, ha ha ha.'

She wished she hadn't come and had stayed where Pam lay on the red couch watching The Avengers.

'What's the matter with old Sid then?'

'Nothing. I'm just thinking.' She lit the cellophane wrapper from a cigarette packet with her cigarette in the ashtray and it flared up then died and was removed by a waitress. Suddenly she got up and said to Joyce, 'I just remembered I have to make a phone call, I'll see you later,' and went out through the plate-glass door into the glassy stare of a psychopath, past his grabbing hand and ran down Earls Court Road. When she got in Pam was not reclining but standing at the ironing board with rollers in her hair and a hideous towel turban. Mrs Gale, with wavy lines distorting her black leather, was throwing men over her shoulder on television.

'The horizontal hold's slipped again.'

'Oh.'

'Hit it, will you? Thanks.'

The flex of the iron grated on the asbestos.

'What brings you back?'

'No reason.'

'Do you think you could sort out the woolies and put them over there?'

She sat down on the edge of the sofa and started separating the little clothes and an occasional stained sock of Lenny's. Pam acted on her like a speech impediment. After some minutes she said:

'Are nylon socks woolies?'

'Thank God I've nearly finished.' Pam sprayed a T-shirt with water and unplugged the iron. 'Now we can relax. I'll just hang up his lordship's shirt.'

She sat beside her, arm along the back of the sofa, and kicked off her shoes; her legs were bare, her toe-nails coral mist on the right, chipped blue pearl on the left.

She put her arm round Sidonie's shoulder so that she fell back against her.

'Comfortable?'

'Yes.' She moved her aching neck and Pam's hair fell on her shoulder and later Pam lay on the red sofa, like a flower beneath her hand.

Not long afterwards, before Pam and Sidonie had admitted that silence crystallized between them in rooms, at the end of an evening's ironing Lenny came in with a member of his sales team. They took off their coats and sat down to talk about money while the macaroni softened upstairs and the rainy sky was suddenly washed with violet.

Pam's jeans had gone to jodhpurs at the knee and her blouse was sleeveless cotton with revers. Sidonie managed to turn the face evaporating in a cloud of steam towards her but macaroni came first. When they went downstairs Joyce was there and sat between Lenny and Sidonie on the sofa; the fellow traveller was in a chair beside them and opposite was Pam, isolated across plates floating like icebergs in the dense dusk.

Half an hour passed and the talk turned from money.

'Poles are the best lovers,' said Lenny's friend.

'You're a good lover, aren't you, darling?' said Pam

to Lenny who did not answer but was smirking in his cup.

Sidonie left the room and stayed upstairs for half an hour. When Pam came up to see what was the matter, they went to the attic where, in the darkness on the rags of a patch-work quilt Sidonie held her and lay until they heard Joyce rattling the bathroom door and shouting.

'She'll wake the kids,' said Pam and with a quick flick to her skirt was half-way down the stairs.

'Don't tell Lenny,' Sidonie had insisted.

'I've told Lenny,' said Pam three days later as they met briefly in the kitchen looking for toothpaste. 'I just had to.'

'What did he say?'

'He said he guessed anyway. He's very pleased.'

Sidonie could not go back downstairs. The next morning after Joyce had left and she was reading on her bed Lenny came in and asked her to go out for a drink. The pub had just opened and was almost empty; Lenny ordered two J.C.'s.

'I'm very pleased about you and Pam, dear.'

'Why?'

'You're the only friend she's got with a mind. Cigarette?'

'I'm not a friend. She doesn't like me.'

'Nonsense, dear.'

He had drunk his beer in one gulp and waited till she finished hers before getting another round.

'Don't hurt her, dear.'

'As if I would. I'd rather – as if I would – '

'All right, dear, I'm sorry. I know you wouldn't purposely. There's just one thing I regret – that it isn't me.' He wiped the froth from his lip. 'Just old Beacon's luck.'

As they left the pub, he said, 'Feel better now you've talked to me?'

'That Joyce is getting too inquisitive,' said Lenny, as he came into the bedroom.

'She isn't,' Sidonie said.

'She hates to be left out of anything, and she senses something's going on that she doesn't know about,' said Pam.

'She follows you two around like a bloodhound.'

'You're imagining it. It's only natural she expects me to go to bed the same time as her.'

'Isn't she loyal, Pam?'

'Joyce is a nosey cow.'

'She isn't,' but if Pam said so, she must be.

Despite Lenny's sneers she dressed under the bed-clothes and went upstairs; Joyce had fallen asleep with the light on.

Lenny would stay for hours in her room talking while she begged him to go and Pam swept loudly outside the door. If she went into the kitchen he followed. The invitations to the bedroom became less frequent after Lenny, feverish and heating the bed like a furnace, begged to lie in the middle and whimpered and cried when Sidonie tried to remove his sweating leg.

'Do you want to go to the shops with Pam?'

'No, thank you.'

Pam and Lenny both looked hurt, so she ran after her, but although she put her hand on the pram, her mouth soon dried and they both wondered why she had come. They came out of the glare into the supermarket and Pam took a silver wire basket and walked past the fresh vegetables to the cold breath of the fridge where their heads were reflected together in the glass above. Pam ran round the shelves like a hen and bumped into her as she doubled back and there was one person too many in the queue at the cash desk.

Between breakfast and washing up, about twelve, Pam or Lenny would make coffee and children climbed

over Lenny's back or the table, burning their feet in
coffee and their fingers on cigarette-ends while they
drank it. Pam finished hers first and Sidonie, making a
cigarette last as long as possible, sat opposite Lenny,
picking the loose formica or drawing in spilt coffee.
When the filter went out she said, 'Can I do anything to
help you, Pam?'

'It's all right. I'll just take down the rubbish, then I'll
start getting lunch,' and she swept vigorously round
their feet.

'If you would just tell me what to do I'll do it,' said
Sidonie in bed but she never did and Lenny would
keep her talking while Pam rattled the reproachful
dustpan.

One hot afternoon at 2.30 walking along West
Cromwell Road, Sidonie and Pam passed a man in a
knitted cap who said, 'You cannot imagine the intoler-
able agony when they stick the lighted matches between
your toes.'

They went into a chemist's and while waiting in the
queue Pam fingered baby foods and gazed longingly at
hair rinses.

'My husband would kill me,' she said to the assistant.
When they got in Pam sidled up to Lenny and put her
arms round him.

'Darling, I've got something to ask you . . .'

'What?' he shrugged her off.

'You'll never let me . . .'

'Get on with it.'

'All right. Don't be angry, darling. I want to rinse my hair – not dye it, only rinse it, can I, darling?'

'I don't care what you do with it.'

In the shop next day she said, 'I'm going to be a devil' to the assistant, who did not know what she was talking about.

Under their gaze an incipient spot could turn to acne. When the washing machine thumped and flooded the kitchen, Lenny searched her cupboard lest she had concealed dirty clothes. The three of them, sometimes separated by Joyce or visitors but always aware, lived in torrid silence, blows and apologies on the splintering second floor. A child, pulling a long sock to his knee in the 90° afternoon, asked if he could go to school tomorrow. He was told 'Of course'; he had mumps, but Pam and Lenny had forgotten. At four o'clock Pam cleared away the lunch things and went to collect the children, who stood, sudden rain beating through cotton dresses, alone outside the empty school. When they got home they were soaked; Lenny prescribed hot milk. They gave him a typed request for arrears of dinner money; he replied with what he called a stinker. After tea he and Pam reduced them to tears by an obsolete method of doing sums. Of Pam's childhood Sidonie learned one night. The baby, fresh from its mother's womb, legs flopping from a lace nightgown, grew into the child with gappy teeth, the bow from whose hair blew for ever over a white sea petrified by the box camera. She had dropped a sewing machine on her foot, had scarlet fever, been interfered with by a man and liked it, passed the 11 plus, passed out at a Guide rally, passed School Certificate.

'How many men have you slept with besides Lenny?'
'Only Lenny.'

She didn't know whether she was disappointed or pleased, but learned later this was irrelevant. Pam had thought she said 'lived'. Because Pam was not a skivvy, even after a quarrel, at supper time Sidonie had to follow her to the kitchen, her longing for words filling her head like a fog. Paralysed against the draining board, shuffling from inch to inch of the floor, she might tentatively get knives and forks from the drawer, but always feared Pam might say, 'What makes you think you're having any?' Sometimes Pam carried everything down herself, so she had to follow unnecessary and empty-handed and Lenny, smacking his lips at food or legs, or ignoring it to punish them, would accuse Pam of officiousness or Sidonie of laziness or let the cat eat his.

At all times Sidonie longed to touch Pam's hips efficient in a grey skirt, her whistling lips, her busy hands, but awed by non-stick saucepans, cheese flaps, graters and spoons, instead wondered whether to put salt and pepper on the tray.

Promptly after tea each evening one of the children would cry: 'We're not going to have any horrid medicine,' reminding their mother who would have forgotten, and 'Not fair,' sucking a spoon wet from a brother's lips into an eager mouth and grimacing.

Sometimes at nightfall or in a storm, as autumn became cold, Earls Court Road seemed to steam; dark faces suddenly flashing in doorways, hands, whistles, cars stopping, breath hanging in the air above groups on the pavement or a snatch of perfume from people hurrying to cold orgies by the electric fire. At Penge she searched her parents' faces for a trace of lust.

'A letter came for you,' said Lenny. 'I took the liberty of sending it back unopened.'

Sidonie had met a boy in the street and agreed to meet him, not intending to go, but during a row had told Pam.

Pam came into the kitchen and dumped the paper

supermarket sack. Lenny was saying to Sidonie, as she put her arms into the sleeves of her coat, 'What's this dreamboat like then?'

'He's small and dark, about two inches taller than me.'

'With a beard?' said Pam.

'Yes, a little one.'

'Oh my God, not that! I just passed him in the road.'

Sidonie grabbed her purse and ran out before Pam's words could hurt her, and tried to forget them as she ran down the street to where Jimmy leant in an off-white mac against a dirty white pillar.

'Sorry I'm late.'

'It's a lady's prerogative or something. What would you like to do?'

'Oh I don't know. Anything nice.'

'What's nice?'

'I don't know.'

'Tell you what: I want to just pop into the Coleherne to see if a guy I know's there; he owes me some bread.'

He wasn't, but they sat down and Jimmy brought two halves of bitter and put them on the table beside his five-Weights pack. After the beer they did not have another because Sidonie felt awkward, as she was the only girl in the bar. Someone was playing the piano.

'This cat also stole a Coltrane album of mine and some

clothes.' She had noticed, when he took off his coat, that his thin body was wearing a pale blue polo-neck sweater that could have belonged to a girl.

'Let's go.' He put on his mac and buttoned it. Then they stepped outside into wind and thick drops of rain from the still-light sky, and got a train to Leicester Square and walked around.

'Do you smoke?'

'Yes. Oh, smoke! Not now. Why, got any?'

'No.'

He laughed, had nice teeth, and did not know the Beacons existed. They went into a pub, Sidonie feeling young and a girl.

He came back from the bar. 'Hey, like a short?'

'Can you?'

'Just about. Got any bread, just in case we run out?'

'Yes, a bit.'

It was so long since she had heard anyone say bread that she hesitated a second, seeing slabs of French bread and cheese with Brother Bung onions on the counter.

Golden and innocuous in her glass, she sipped the whisky and a bitter chaser. The pub was filling up and an old lady was singing the old songs. Jimmy had bought another, but not one for himself. 'I'll skip this round. I get stoned on wine gums.' He held her free hand and

between drags of the shared cigarette, told her he was
an illegitimate orphan who had lived in London all his
life.

'Are you a good drummer?'

'I should practise.'

'Practise makes perfect.'

'Mentally I am perfect. It's just sometimes my hands.'

A friend of Jimmy had come in and joined them,
blond beautiful, with a scattering of spots.

'I just ran into Jean.'

'Where?'

'She says she's going to the all-nighter. She's looking
for you to scratch out those pretty brown eyes.'

'Thanks.'

'Who's Jean?'

'Some crazy chick.'

When Jimmy was away making a phone call or in
the gents:

'Who's Jean?'

'His bird.'

'He's not married to her, is he?'

'No. They've just been together for about four years
though. I shouldn't have told you, should I?'

'It's nothing to me,' which was true. What seemed
more important was the pattern of his trousers.

'Look.' She pointed to her knee and then to his.

'What?'

'Your trousers are the exact same identical material as my skirt.'

'We've got something in common.'

'Aren't you observant?'

'You're worth observing.'

Jimmy came back and picked up his mac and said, 'Coming, Sidonie?'

'What's the hurry, all of a sudden?'

'I asked her if she was coming.'

'Yes, if you are.'

He walked ahead of her in the rain.

'What's the matter, Jimmy? What's the hurry? Something wrong?'

'I don't like you talking to that bastard.'

'It didn't mean anything, darling, we were just talking.'

She put her arm through his and although she was talking to lost Lewis and he to hunting Jean, they walked together in a united glow and Jimmy held the door open for Sidonie as they entered the dark light of the next pub.

Now he had Sidonie's money and bought some cigarettes. Sounds of voices, glass and money became the substance and then the background of her thoughts, and then she didn't have any thoughts, only eyes watching the drift of smoke.

'You look brought down about something.'

'On the contrary. I am content.'

'I feel like dancing, do you feel like dancing? It's in my blood – look, I can't stop my feet from dancing.' His feet jigged monotonously in unpolished boots. 'Do you feel like dancing?'

'Maybe a bit later,' when the Beacons are finally drowned.

Happiness hit her. As they sat she smiled at him as at her only true love.

'Wow! That smile does things to me. You know, when you smile you really look like an angel.'

The hands of the clock had moved to five past ten – she drained the glass of golden whisky, which, poured into its works, would halt them but down her throat would not.

'Who's Jean?' she asked. But he didn't hear and she remembered what he said about wine gums. She saw his Caribbean eyelashes curling backwards and felt their hands sweating together under the table. In the ladies, in the mirror, she tried to solidify with cold water her face which was disintegrating, and when her eyes were back in focus and their appointed sockets, went down the carpeted stairs past naked stares back to the table.

'Hey, listen.' They were out in the street now, and Jimmy had fallen down twice already and grabbed her arm, pulling her down with him into the wet black gutter near the wheels of a stationary vehicle. Men were standing round or faces. They got up, Jimmy with a wet black smear on the back of his mac. Sidonie looked down at her mud-splashed legs, blood, mud an incipient ladder, and forgot them. Then jokes and the lights, and the rain, then they were on the platform and in a train.

I hope it doesn't wear off before I get home, thought Sidonie, because if she saw the Beacons it would give her courage and if she went to bed, sleep. She wondered why they were going home so early and remembered Jean and was satisfied because she didn't want complications with Jimmy. Coming down the road, he asked if she was going to ask him in, and she said she would, only her friend was ill and would be in bed, and then threw her arms round his neck. 'You do understand, darling, don't you?' He was running up and down the wet steps chasing her round the pillars of a house, when she stopped in a scream of laughter; on the opposite side of the road were two linked figures, a sinister floral skirt.

Then they were gone, but not before two white faces accused through the rain.

'Let's go for a walk,' she said but feet were impelled back to the dark green door whose number was falling from the cracked pillar. But before they arrived, hatless and hairless and not less sinister than if headless in the rain, a figure passed them and said out of its face. 'You're as pissed as a newt.'

When she managed to get in out of the ruins of the evening, there were footsteps on the stairs behind her and before she locked her door she heard '. . . after her like that – she's old enough to take care of herself.'

'I feel responsible – if anything happened – '

'Pull the other one – '

'All right. If you want a row, I'm quite willing.'

'No. I'm sorry, Lenny, sorry.'

The words hung in the darkness; she switched on the light. Joyce lay on the pillow inhaling a mouthful of sheet. Sidonie lay down without taking her clothes off, the electric light burned eight inches from the ceiling and burned her eyes till the Beacons battered at the door, 'Let us in.'

She finally did and focused on the light, while they whispered accusations and the room went round; an occasional word battered itself against the bulb and disintegrated. Kissing, disgusting, arms round his neck, practically raping, pissed. She sensed Lenny's hand was too near the switch and could plunge the room in darkness where their words could form battalions and converge. But they went, leaving two columns of alien air in the corner by the door. Now a moth was beating round the bulb and she switched off the light and groped to bed with tiny suns and planets wheeling in front of her eyes.

'How do you think Pam felt, seeing you kissing him like that? She's got feelings too, you know.'

'Has she?'

He put down the accusing Rice Krispies and tea and banged some down beside Joyce's bed and she sat up and stirred them sleepily with the spoon. The door opened and Pam's teeth and gums flashed from the doorway.

'Yes, I have got feelings.' And the door banged.

'What's all that in aid of?'

'Something to do with Rice Krispies, I expect. It annoys her when Lenny brings in our breakfast.'

'What's the clock say? – apart from tick tock.'

'Eleven. It's Saturday.'

'O.K. Beacon, let's have the next course,' said Joyce, and was not quelled by his stare, as he kicked open the

door in time to hear, and laid eggs and toast beside each
bed.

'Did I hear someone call me a stupid git?' reappearing
in the door.

'No. No.'

'Just be very careful, that's all.'

The following morning, a grey Sunday, they waited
in vain for breakfast in bed. Joyce optimistically gave it
till one, then at two, just before hunger compelled them
to go out Jimmy called. He did not stay long and
arranged to meet her the following Tuesday, which was
reported by a relay of blue-nosed spies peeping through
the adjoining door of their unheated room.

At tea, to which she and Joyce were invited by Lenny,
and they suspected, not by Pam, he said, 'Where does
Jimmy live?'

'Bayswater.'

'Why doesn't he get a flat nearer here?'

'Why?'

'Save fares. Why doesn't he just move in here alto-
gether?'

'Why are you getting all bitter and twisted about
him?' said Joyce, emptying her cup for more tea.

'There's nothing twisted about Lenny, he's quite
straight,' said Pam and laughed. 'Oh well, I thought it

was funny anyway, ha, ha, ha!' and slammed the teapot on the stove. 'Anyone who wants more tea can get it themselves. I'm tired of being the only waitress.'

'Pam. Sit down. You will apologise for your bad temper in front of the children.'

She slumped, crashed, 'Oh I apologise, children dear, for complaining. Satisfied?'

'Pam – I am going to lose my temper in a minute.'

'I'm sorry. More tea, darling?'

'I'll get it myself. Sit down.'

'Mummy's naughty, isn't she?'

'Yes, dear.'

Then that same child dropped a plate and was banished.

Lenny belched through the festive season. Money had been borrowed at five o'clock on Christmas Eve to buy each of the children a present; he had abandoned the idea of making a steam-roller from seven-pint beer cans. Pam, a slash of green, was very very drunk. Pine needles caught in her green dress and rattled on the wooden floor as she danced to the record for the twentieth time.

> '. . . just like the ones we used to know,
> Where the tree-tops glisten
> And children listen
> To hear the sleigh bells in the snow . . .'

while fog massed outside and the Beacon children, ears deadened to the noise, slept with no stockings dangling from mantelpiece or bed. Six or seven people in varying degrees of drunkenness danced in paper hats; a spark from a cracker had burned Lenny's eye; to the Beacons this was a family Christmas but Sidonie wanted her own.

There was a shriek from the bedroom and Pam bounded back and threw her arms round Lenny.

'Oh, darling, aren't you gorgeous! Aren't you sweet! He's nailed a bit of mistletoe above the bed!'

'You put it there this afternoon.'

Sidonie had met Joyce at lunch-time in a Holborn pub hung with lights and decorations, and crowds of office workers were swelling on to the street. When she came home from the office party at half past eight, loaded with presents and vodka and lime, Sidonie went with her to Liverpool Street Station and watched the train heave through the darkness towards lights and home, then turned back down the littered steps into the raw light of the Underground. She had wanted to go home on the morning of Christmas Eve.

'Don't you want to be with us, darlin'?'

'Christmas is for families.'

'You're part of our family now.'

When she had insisted on going to Penge on Christmas Day he said, 'Why not ask your Mum and Dad up here for Christmas? Make a change for them.'

'Why on earth do you want to spend Christmas Eve with those terrible people?' her mother had asked, putting mince-pies into the oven and adjusting the temperature with floury hands. Relations were expected over the holiday.

'Get six packets of Lyons mince-pies,' said Lenny to Pam who was making a list, 'and two Christmas puddings.' He begged a turkey from a customer, the wife of a butcher, and when she had taken him to the shop one evening in her husband's absence, chose an angry looking pink giant and had her remove the gaunt claws and wrap it, and arrived home much later with sawdust on his hair and knees.

The children had brought home from school paper Father Christmases with expanding legs, crayoned in scratchy red and black, and these drooped round the kitchen or hung on the wall, a pin through their heads, legs dangling and shaking palsiedly when the door was opened. They had been asked at school to ask their mummies to give them something for the Christmas party, but Pam had not seen why the parents should provide it so after many tears they were allowed a packet of biscuits among them. They were asked to several parties, to which they went if Pam remembered or lunch had not got too late. The cold smell of decay drifted up from the dustbins in the basement through the bars of their windows, and Lenny, to silence Pam, went down armed with a defunct flit spray and called Sidonie to come with him. Pam shouted something after them, suspecting at least a kiss in the cobwebs, if not passion on wet newspaper. At the back of the dark cave which stretched beneath the pavement, behind the row of bins stood a dustbin by itself where the dustmen did not penetrate. Festoons of mould and fungus hung green in torchlight across the bulging rim and down the sides; the lid lay beside it. Lenny, playing the beam round the floor, suddenly jumped back, his feet grating on glass, and grabbing Sidonie's arm, exposed a nest of full grown rats glaring in the light. For a minute they lay staring at him, then one leaped into the open dustbin and the rest scattered. Lenny seized the dustbin and stood legs apart, pouring his cornucopia of filth on to the floor. The rat disappeared and Lenny bent down to scrape up the rubbish; Sidonie lifted two or three egg-shells between finger and thumb and pushed the dustbin to the front of the cellar. They decided not to mention the rats, as Pam would panic, and it was unlikely they would reach the second floor.

'None of you children are to go in the cellar,' said Lenny, washing his hands.

'Why not?'

'Because I said so.'

'Why?'

'Because there are great big rats that bite your throat out,' said Sidonie.

'Of course there aren't,' said Pam. 'The only rats in this house are upstairs.'

But one of the children, a sensitive boy who had that morning opened a new railway across his sister's face with a metal train, had to be held sobbing in Lenny's arms for many nights to come, as he woke from dreams of giant rats.

The morning Pam bought the rat poison there was no breakfast, and the morning they found a glazed rat, half-way up the stairs, splinters of lino in its teeth, no one felt like eating.

In abortive attempts to fool the National Insurance people, Lenny had been using the alias Leslie Bacon, and came stumbling upstairs holding by its torn corner a brown enveloped containing a summons addressed to Leonard Batewell. Pam retrieved it from the wastebin under the sink and propped it, now stained from a dripping eggshell, on the dresser, where it stood until two officials called. A week later Lenny appeared at the magistrates court with four of the children and was ordered to pay at the rate of two pounds a week. Pam and Lenny had been telling their friends that Lenny faced certain imprisonment and bore their disappointment well.

Sidonie had solved the problem of Pam's Christmas present by giving her nothing. This solution rankled, but she had no money and feared to go to the Labour Exchange because her card was not properly stamped. Pam had grown less beautiful; perhaps it was just her fading tan and frequent tears. Sidonie longed to comfort her, but had no words to speak to a housewife. Outside the house, Pam was brash and engaged the green-grocer in ribaldry. She had also lost some weight and was constantly plucking at the waist band of her skirt.

'I could kill Lenny,' she said to Joyce and Sidonie. 'He'll give his money away to any Tom, Dick and Harry with a hard-luck story. Never mind if his own wife and children starve.'

Sidonie left the room as soon as possible; she had given Pam some money she had received for Christmas. Later, she went shopping with her. Hearing cries from the pram outside, Pam finished laughing and said to the greengrocer, 'Oh well, must get home to feed all my monsters. Small packet of frozen peas, please.'

Lenny stayed at home with an alleged headache and a miserable evening's viewing killed the hours until one of Lenny's team called and Lenny hid in the bedroom. Pam sat rubbing her eyebrow with her finger while the man talked.

'Lenny's managed to break me of most of my habits,' she said, stopping herself.

'I don't know what's got into Lenny lately,' said his friend. 'He used to be a hard man, now he's soft. Something rotten's got into him. No offence, Pam.'

'More tea anyone?' replied Pam, but the pot was empty and she went out to pour hot water on the stewed leaves.

'I think perhaps you know what I meant,' said Lenny's friend to Sidonie. 'Pam's a clever little actress, you know.'

'What?' said Sidonie, very frightened, but Pam came back and the friend left.

Lenny put on some records and started to dance, but nobody liked each other much without alcohol and the people in the basement came to complain of music upstairs.

'I'm going down the road. Shall I get you a paper?'

'Oh – well, I was just going to get one.'

'I might as well get it.'

Pam closed the door and Sidonie turned back to the gas fire, changing her position on the hard carpet when her knees grew red from the heat. When the paper came it was the *Standard* as well as the *News*. She spread them out and read all the news and sport before turning to the Situations columns. She was not experienced, smart, keen, capable, male or disabled, which left her a limited selection. Every morning Pam gave her the papers and some mornings she could restrain her tears. As she leaned over the table and Pam checked that there was nothing, the print blurred and doubled and children yelled as she went back to the bedroom fit for nothing, or ate their food at their insistence.

'Why don't you go to an agency? It's the simplest thing.'

'Yes.'

She couldn't enter an agency or supply credentials to the capable ladies behind the desks and her greatest fear was that if she went Pam would accompany her. When Lenny came into her room, she quickly turned to Office Vacancies and he underlined suitable jobs in biro and offered to phone to make appointments, and Pam, dustpan or child in hand, was furious to find them together.

'The simplest thing would be to go to an agency,' pushing back her hair, leaving a coal streak on her forehead.

'I'm going to – this afternoon.'

'Well, which one will you try?'

'Oh, I don't know, there's hundreds in Oxford Street.'

'There must be one locally.'

'It doesn't matter, does it? They're all agencies.'

'It just seems bloody stupid to go right up to Oxford Street when you could get one locally.'

Lenny, who had gone out, came back with a telephone directory, leaving the door open so that children got in and jumped in shoes on the made beds.

'If you make a list of a few local agencies you'll know where to start, else you'll be poncing about all afternoon.'

She nodded and took the book with weak hands, her fingers fluttering the pages.

'I can't possibly read it with those kids in here!'

'No need to lose your temper.'

'We're not going out, are we, Daddy?'

'You have exactly five to get out. One-two-three-four-five.'

'Oh well, I've got work to do, if no one else has,' said Pam, and as Lenny did not detain her, she had to go.

'Now you get out too.'

'Darlin' – it's not me who wants you to get a job. I
hate to do this to you?'

'Get out then.'

He put his hand on her shoulder but it was shrugged
off with venom and he went out, banging the door. She
rocked back and forwards on the floor with her arms
round her head, saying, 'I can't possibly. I can't.'

The door opened and Pam said:

'What have you done to offend Lenny?'

'Nothing.'

'Well you'd better apologise anyway. I don't see why
you have to be so offensive all the time.'

'It's not my fault if he takes offence at nothing.'

'Lenny is the most easy-going person I know. Unless
you want to make things unpleasant for all of us, I
suggest you apologise.'

After a bit she got up and went into the kitchen.

'I'm sorry.'

'What for?'

'Offending you.'

'You don't mean it. You're not really sorry at all. I
can see the old hate in your eyes, Sidonie.'

'All right, I'm not then. I only said it because bloody
Pam told me to.'

He turned to Pam.

'Why don't you keep your ugly face out of things that don't concern you?'

'I was only trying to sort things out.'

They both turned to march out of the kitchen and collided in the doorway. Lenny rushed back in and crashed his fist on the table.

'I apologise,' he screamed.

Sidonie ran downstairs.

'Where are you going?'

'To an agency.'

'Have you got a list?'

'What about lunch?' shouted Pam over the bannisters.

'You know what you can do with your lunch.'

When she was half-way up Earls Court Road, she slowed down, having no list in her pocket and nowhere to go.

The smog grew worse towards Notting Hill and people were bumping through the streets with pads over their mouths and noses – Sidonie had imagined a smog mask as a great rubber obsolescence – and scarves and collars pulled up as pallid electric lights swam in the thick grey air. Sidonie spent half an hour in W. H. Smith's reading paperbacks, and thinking she had been there at least an hour, emerged through glass doors into night at three o'clock.

'I've been watching you wandering about. Would you like a coffee?'

She turned and saw a West Indian face, white teeth unmasked in the smog.

'I thought you meant in a coffee bar,' she said, as he ran up the decaying steps of a great divided house where fungus grew round the swollen list of residents. She followed him up to a room on the top floor – green case on top of the wardrobe, self-portrait in Kodachrome on the mantelpiece, gas fire, sagging moquette chair, and dirty yellow candlewick bedspread on the bed.

'Would you like me to do anything?' she asked when he started to take cups and saucers from the cupboard.

'You can make it if you like.'

The spoon sank voluptuously through broken foil into a full tin of coffee. The sugar was standing on a pile of books on economics. As she sat opposite him in that high room, eating fruitcake out of a tin, with nothing to look forward to, he put on a record. 'Like to dance?'

She did, adjusting her skirt in the mirror, and when he started kissing her was resigned, but suddenly was able to break away and walked down Church Street and along the High Street to the school, where Pam waited alone, the children having been let out early and the other mothers anticipating or knowing it.

'Well, I've got a job. Nine pounds ten. Start on Monday. Nine-thirty to five.'

'I told you to go to an agency, didn't I?'

After waiting another ten minutes Pam went into the playground and was informed by a cleaner that every one had left half an hour ago. She broke the good news to Lenny, who had made the tea, and the children who sat already stuffed and smeared with jam round the table, coats and satchels in a pile of coal-dust by the stove. This stove was the cause of many bitter scenes, because Lenny would say he was getting the coal, and as the room grew cold and the ashes sagged, Pam would grab the bucket and march efficiently to the cellar, only to have Lenny rush after her and tear it from her hand and throw it or her downstairs; or he would silently let her scrabble and wonder all evening what she had done wrong. Sidonie described her interview and gave the name of the firm.

'I'll be able to pay the back rent I owe.'

'Perhaps the children can have some shoes now,' said Pam, 'I see there's another sale at Pontings . . .'

'If the children need shoes, the children get shoes,' said Lenny and could not be prevailed upon to have any tea.

Pam cried till she saw a crumby plate and tea-stained mug in the sink.

On Monday morning Sidonie got up at eight with

Joyce and went into the kitchen and was surprised to see
Pam and Lenny already up.

The wireless was playing very loud and dressing
gowns draped their unwashed bodies as Pam guarded
the door while Lenny prodded a knife into the bent
mouths of the children's money boxes. A little heap of
pennies and halfpennies lay on the table. Both Beacons
looked very guilty. At breakfast one of the girls asked,
'Why aren't we having eggs?'

'We can't afford any, darling.'

'Mummy, you can have all the money in my money
box.'

'Shut up and eat your cereal,' said Lenny.

Sidonie borrowed half a crown from Joyce, who was
pleased she was working again. At the station they got
on the same train, but when Joyce got off at Piccadilly
Sidonie stayed on to Holborn and, after changing lines
from blue to brown to purple, got out at Goldhawk
Road Station. Slush stained her shoes as she walked along
and accumulated under soggy stockings as she stood at
the coffee stall at the entrance to the market. Then suddenly there were sherry coloured eyes through a bunch
of necklaces, face corrugated by a birdcage, checked coat
behind a curtain of chickens and feathers, foul breath
on the broiler fowls, as Lenny Beacon with the relent-

lessness of love, pursued her through Shepherd's Bush market. Running along the street her heel caught in a crack with a wrench across her foot, and she stopped to see him standing in a doorway, wiping his skull. He picked up her shoe.

'Needs heeling as well now,' and handed it to her.

'Why did you lie to me?'

She put it on and kicked him.

'You filthy spy.'

'Being offensive isn't going to do any good. You're in the wrong, Sidonie, and you know it.'

The drops from a folded awning fell on his head and he moved out on to the pavement.

'Let's get out of here,' as a rusty drip fell past his ear.

'I'm not going with you,' although his fingers were like pincers in her wet sleeve: and they walked until they came to a café, where she sat catatonically, her thoughts going no further than the white cup of tea with two sugars, knowing that if her mind moved a fraction she would be aware of the terrible inescapability from Beacon and the years of hours of evasion to the end – a grave or funeral being inconceivable – the end was a tangled bed or a floor in an empty room.

Lenny was speaking and she didn't hear his words.

'Why am I so self-absorbed?' Before the thought was complete it sank below the surface, where dreams writhed, remembered by the eyes as red and green churning in black. The beautiful tea was burning her hands through the white cup; she held them there. Lenny is lighting a cigarette, drawing it in through his pretty mouth and exhaling. He rasps his hand over his unshaven cheek and chases a bit of tobacco over uncleaned teeth with his tongue. He stops talking and dips his lip into the cup, sucking up a mouthful of salutary tea that floats the particles from between his teeth and the nicotine from his tongue. She is drawing a picture in the ashtray with a match and doesn't answer because it is important that the sides of the volcano slope evenly; the grey dust silts slowly over his raw words and when they are covered, she makes a flower of raw tobacco shreds.

'Lied to me – why? Why? The least you could do. Pam – lied to me – why? Pam. Pam – why to me?'

'I don't know.'

One petal was longer than the others and the match slipped, spoiling its neighbour. She mends and tends the broken petals and a drip from her cup has swamped the volcano and irrigated the flower and another falls so the petals float in confusion in a mesh of ash. Her neck aches as she looks up into Lenny's eyes, immobile above the white rim. It is all right in the café, it's warm and secure although made temporary by the clock on the wall. Three red plastic carnations stand in a vase on the counter with a yellow daffodil, yellower than sunshine and sunlight soap rubbed by hacked hands over shirt collars, black with two days' wear, despite detergents and soapflakes, the winner of a washing competition, her mother's mother long decayed in the long graveyard at St Mary Cray, visible from the windows of the Catford loop line train. Lenny gets up, walks to the door, is inches from it and turns with two cups of tea in his hand.

'What are you going to say to Pam?'

'Nothing. What are you?'

'Naturally, I shall try to make her see it from your point of view. Look, Sidonie, I didn't want you to get a job. Why did you do it, dear, it was very naughty of you, wasn't it?'

'I want one of those cakes.'

'Which, darlin', custard tarts?'

'The ones with white strips.'

When he brought it, he was still stern but she wasn't afraid, until they had passed Gloucester Road on the train and he sat opposite her planning the words for her betrayal.

'Don't tell Pam.'

'I'll have to.'

'No, you won't. I'll get a job tomorrow.'

'You won't start till Monday even if you do. What about the rent?'

'I'll borrow it from someone. Please, Lenny, don't tell her. You know what she'll be like.'

'All right, I won't tell her. You will though. I'll give you until I get in tonight.'

'Oh thank you, Lenny. This is where you get out. don't know how to thank you, so I won't try. Good-bye.'

She gave him a push but he sat until the doors closed.

'I'm not going to let you ponce about on your own all day. We'll go and have a drink somewhere.'

Later, feeling warm, the water flowing unnoticed through her shoes, they went to the cinema and watched naked girls play table tennis, the soles of their arched feet facing the camera, and with immaculate make-up, play with beachballs in a swimming pool.

Lenny went in ten minutes before her and she dialled TIM in a phone box and was told it was six o'clock. Tea was over when she came in and Pam too preoccupied with the baby to pay much attention to the answers to her verbal questionnaire. Lenny, seated at the head of the table, asked if the boss had made a pass at her. She had a piece of bread and raspberry jam and tea heated by water from the kettle boiling for the baby's bottle. In spite of the month and the weather, Pam's shoulders were obscured by a red angora sweater, but her arms were exposed white against the baby's skin; and the kitchen was hot, her lips were bare and only black pencil showed round her eyes. It was when her mouth was absorbed and her eyes otherwise engaged that Sidonie wanted to kiss her most and until she spoke could watch unnoticed over cigarette smoke. When she did speak, Sidonie heard her answering voice go more suburban and felt her face pale and redden. The way Pam clicked the fastening on the plastic pants and picked up the smouldering paddi pants with zinc-and-castor-oil ointment on her fingers showed she was assessing the unwashed dishes. Sidonie, after standing like a cipher at the draining board, filled the bowl with water and stood in front of the sink with her back exposed to Pam, who was not looking at her. As she scraped hardened Farex from a spoon she saw she had used Fairy Snow instead of Daz and ran the cold tap lest, this being unnoticed, she be accused of not rinsing.

'I don't know how she does it! You've flooded the place.'

There were a few splashes on the floor; Lenny had come into the room.

'How's the old wage-earner, then? How's it feel to be a working girl again, eh?'

He came up behind her, tickling her waist, and when she shrugged him off, grabbed her wrists with one hand and held her hands in the water, tickling her with the other. She screamed; he had driven a blunt knife into her hand.

'Let go you sod, Lenny, for Christ's sake let go.'

'Foul language eh? That deserves a little tickle, don't you think, Pam?'

'Don't ask me.'

'Now, Pam, let's not start, shall we?'

'Lenny, will you let go – you're stabbing me, let go of my wrist.'

'What's this? Tears of temper in the old eyes?'

'I've got a knife in my hand.' She kicked him and he let her go and she brought up her hand dripping blood and bubbles.

'Oh my God, Sidonie, sit down quick. Pam! Where's the plaster?'

'In the cupboard, of course. Top shelf.'

As she sat with Lenny anointing and apologising and trimming the plaster, she thought she might faint but couldn't. If it had been my side or stomach – white walls, tubes and needles an unhumiliating release, days of anaesthetized sleep, long days of convalescence by the tossing Atlantic, the salt wind lifting heavy hair, and seaweed on the rocks. But Lenny was already telling her to hold her hand in the air and smoothing the last edge over the wound which, as Pam said, was not very deep and a clean cut.

Lenny finished the washing up.

'Darlin', have you been using Fairy Snow?'

'No.'

'Are you sure? The water feels very slimy.'

'If I had it would be green, and it's blue, isn't it, which proves I used Daz.'

'Grey.'

'All right. I used Fairy Snow. Is that what you want me to say? I didn't really take that packet of Daz and pour it into the water, I deliberately used the Fairy Snow because I wasn't washing nappies.'

'Don't be silly, dear.'

'Why bother to lie?' said Pam. 'Why not just admit you used Fairy Snow and have done with it?'

'Yes. Why bother? I used Fairy Snow and Lenny didn't stab my hand.'

Lenny lifted up the bowl and a shower of water and

knives and plates crashed on to the floor and he ran out of the room. The slam of the door echoed in the kitchen, the baby started crying and Pam picked it up.

'That was a damn stupid thing to say,' The water was running towards the legs of her chair. Sidonie wiped it up with her left hand and as she put two halves of a broken plate in the refuse bin, knew a child would cut its fingers on it tomorrow.

She went into her room and heard Joyce's feet on the stairs and her key being shoved in the lock. She came in and kicked off her shoes and flung herself on to the bed. 'What a day!' She was lying face downwards, her blue dress half-way up her thighs and turned over quickly, expecting to be hit when Lenny walked in but he didn't look at her.

'Be like that then. Don't say hello – I don't care.'

'Hello, Joyce.'

He stood breathing, his white face and neck sweating and his torso expanding in his black shirt, then took a cigarette, put it between his lips and lit it.

'Yes thank you, I would like one,' said Joyce and grabbed at one as it hit her in the face.

'What's up with you two?' She made her fingers into a knife and cut the atmosphere, then got up to comb her hair, as they looked only at each other.

'Have you told her?'

'Not yet. Give me time.'

'I'm going out now. I'll be back by eleven.' The door closed, click.

'What's all that about?'

'Nothing.'

'Oh, I almost forgot – how did it go today?'

'Lousy – all right – you know.'

Joyce was getting ready to go out.

'I'm going to dress up all feminine for Bill tonight. This is my beauty routine – first a luxurious bath, then wash and set my hair and do my nails. Oh yes, I've got a face pack. It does two, so you can have half if you like.'

She took off her dress and went into the bathroom in a short white bathrobe and returned immediately for her purse. 'No bloody gas. How can one possibly be expected to be glamorous in such sordid conditions?' Sidonie heard Pam take the baby into the bedroom and shout at the children and knew she would soon be alone downstairs with the television and the ironing board. So she went and knocked on the bathroom door.

'Go away.'

'It's me. Let me in.' Joyce, pink and dripping and clutching a towel, let her into the steamy room. She sat down on the slippery edge of the bath and watched without desire soaped legs and breasts and floating hair and scrubbed the brown back with a loofah and soap and might have been cleaning the bath. Pam, on a July afternoon when green leaves blew across the half-open window, had lain back in the greenish water, long trails of hair floating behind her, her shoulders under water, legs shimmering like reflections, stood up and water pearls and seed pearls of soap rolled down her stomach, placed one foot on the rim and diamonds dissolved in French Fern talc. Then in the kitchen Sidonie had sat on the window-sill while the sun dried marks of wet breasts from her denim shirt, and Pam organized children and bread and butter. Eyes filled with tears as Sidonie, profiteering from the short spell of privilege, lifted the thick crust, yellow with butter and streaked with Marmite, from the bottom of the plate.

Gunfire started from the television downstairs. Joyce drowned it by pulling out the plug. As they stood side by side in the wiped area of the steamed mirror applying the white facepack to their faces, Sidonie felt she was playing at being young, and when Joyce went out stayed in her room, thinking of parties she might have been at, until at half past ten she went downstairs to be there before Lenny.

He came in, his check coat spotted with sleet, and threw his brief-case on to the sofa and thrust his pinched face to the fireguard.

'Well?' He turned to face them. 'What have you been talking about this evening?'

'Are you trying to be funny?' said Pam.

He turned to Sidonie.

'What do you shoot a pink elephant with? A pink elephant gun,' she said quickly.

'What do you shoot a white elephant with?'

'A white elephant gun,' groaned Lenny.

'No. Twist it's tail till it turns pink and shoot it with a pink elephant gun.'

'Hasn't said a damn word all evening.'

'Why do crocodiles wear short pants?'

'So they can get halves on the buses. Sidonie, have you told – ?'

'No, I haven't. Pam, what's grey with four legs and a trunk?'

'An elephant.'

'A mouse going on holiday. What's brown with four legs and a trunk?'

'A mouse coming back from holiday.'

'Ha, ha, ha.'

'I'm going to get supper.' Pam went out.

'Sidonie!'

'What's green and fuzzy and goes up and down?'

She rushed over and gave him a lingering kiss on the lips –

'A gooseberry in a lift' – and ran upstairs and while he was sitting smiling, was scrubbing her mouth with a flannel. In the kitchen she asked Pam, 'Why does the polar bear wear a fur coat?' and was not answered.

'He'd look pretty silly in a plastic mac,' she muttered. She came down pale but whistling with Pam and the supper and the subject of jobs was not mentioned. Lenny had had a bad night, returning with a deficit of two shillings.

'Perhaps there's something wrong with your approach, darling,' suggested Pam, and regretted it when she pulled the splayed sausage from her ear.

'For God's sake do up your blouse,' said Lenny. He got out the scrabble board, but Pam wouldn't play because of a minor disagreement about rules.

'Pam, you will play scrabble and enjoy it.' But she didn't and went to bed, bringing the clock into the sitting-room to wind.

Sidonie went to the kitchen, where dried Rice Krispies lay like leprosy on the floor, to clean her teeth. Lenny stood in the doorway so she hesitated to spit.

'Meet me at the station at ten tomorrow,' he said and leered at her reflection in the mirror.

'Very well.'

It was snowing heavily as they walked round back streets, and were half paralysed when Sidonie remembered the Air Terminal. While they thawed, Lenny began to talk very reasonably about sex; while he was in the gents, Sidonie read an abandoned newspaper. For the next few weeks this was the pattern of their days; they met either at the station or the Terminal, according to how soon Lenny was free; if they had any money, they went to a pub till three, or occasionally had a meal in a café when Lenny got worried about Sidonie's health. He talked about sex every day and hoped Sidonie would come to him with any problems. One bitter afternoon in South Kensington Lenny walked crookedly along a white line in the road, his breath and coat stinking of whisky, while a young constable asked Sidonie if he had been taking drugs. This scared them and they took to avoiding policemen.

Sidonie noticed that the nicer she was to Lenny, the nicer he was to Pam. She felt no guilt.

The snow evaporated. Before meeting Lenny, Sidonie went for a long walk and witnessed a road accident, red blood spattered across a windscreen reflecting the pink

sky. When she reached South Kensington Station she
was an hour late and saw with deep depression the faith-
ful check coat and unsmiling pale face come down the
steps from the arcade towards her.

'What happened to you?'

'What do you mean, what happened? Nothing
happened.'

'You're an hour late.'

'No. You were an hour early.'

'All right, Sidonie, all right.'

'Why are you going down here?'

'I want to phone the office and see if any money's
come in for me.'

'It won't have.'

Lenny held the door of the booth open for her and
shut it behind them. She could hear him breathing.

'If it's of any interest to you, I waited up all night for
you.'

'Well it isn't.'

Lenny picked up the receiver and stood with the dial-
ling tone buzzing in his ear to give an illusion of
normality. Someone had stuck a picture of the Cruci-
fixion on the coinbox; underneath it was written 'Remember that I died for thee'. Lenny picked at it with his
fingers.

'Where did you go last night? You know I'll only be angry for a minute then I'll get over it. Where, darlin'? Why won't you answer my questions? Why? Darlin', look at me! Why?'

His face hovered close to hers and she could feel his knee against her leg.

'Don't breathe on me – you're cutting off my oxygen.'

'What on earth do you mean?'

'I can't breathe with you staring at me like that – can't you open the door or something please – '

'Do you hate me so much then?' in a quiet sorrowful voice.

Sidonie turned her back on him and opened a magazine she had found on the train.

. . . Our unabashed dictionary defines genius as a nudist with a memory for faces.

'Operator! Are you there!'

On the first night of their honeymoon the bride slipped into a flimsy bit of silk and crawled into bed, only to find that her husband had settled down on the couch. When she asked why he was apparently not going to make love to her, he replied, 'Because it's Lent.'

'Why that's the most ridiculous thing I've ever heard,' she exclaimed, almost in tears. *'To whom and for how long?'*

'Operator?'

We know an executive who is so old that when he chases his secretary round the desk, he can't remember why.

She looked at the clock; it was twelve twenty-five and they had been in the phone box for half an hour. She felt sick and said, 'Excuse me, please,' and he said, 'Where are you going?'

'I'll be back in a minute.'

As she went through the barrier and into the ladies, she passed an old woman with a torn plastic shopping bag and tears dribbling from her eyes. All were engaged. The attendant, who had no teeth and wore a grey uniform, was standing outside one of the doors shouting to a friend.

'Did you see what was in her bag they found outside?'

'What?'

'All broken eggshells and matchboxes and bits of bread. Don't know what she wants it all for.'

Laughter came from inside.

'And did you see the ticket she showed old Jim?'

'No.'

'It was like her face – rotten. And black. She's a crafty bitch. When she gets cleared out of here, she goes to Gloucester Road – just goes between the two – never through the barrier.'

The end cell was vacated and Sidonie stood with her forehead against the cold door, where it was not inscribed, and tried not to listen, but could still hear.

'Monday when I was cleaning in here she stood on the mat and wet herself.'

'Dirty cow.'

Sidonie rinsed her hands under the tap, while black hairs fell into the sink from the comb of the woman at the mirror, then she went back. Lenny still had not got through, and she stood with her back to him, looking out, while he alternately dialled and slammed down the receiver.

'Operator! Will you check Grosvenor 4794 and find out if it's engaged or if the line's out of order, thank you!'

People coming through the side entrance with spray on heads and shoulders and shaking umbrellas showed that it was raining again.

'Operator. Is there an alternative number? It's a business line, so there should be,'

He pulled her towards him; she didn't look at him, resting his nose in her face, 'Darlin', why don't you confide in me?' – that nose, raison d'être and ruin of so many man-sized handkerchiefs with a big blue D for Daddy.

Although sitting in the Underground, a little thinner, she gave an impression of toughness, tonight she was

vulnerable and two boys aged about sixteen, sitting on
the long seat, made her blush by looking at her, and
seeing this, stared so that she had to look out of the
window at her smudged face on the black glass, violet
smears under her eyes and dirty rain marks blurring her
skin. She clasped her hands and felt the bones. Opposite
and above her head was the purple map of the new
Victoria Line. The train went slowly, almost stopping
between the stations which followed according to the
map of the Piccadilly Line. She tried to close her eyes but
each station was two minutes nearer standing alone in
the crowded lift, walking through the automatic door,
putting her ticket across arms and faces into the hand of
the ticket collector, and keeping close to shops and
shadows, walking with mascara masking the chaos in the
eyes, then turning her key and forcing the door she least
of all wanted to open.

After a dismal game of three-handed poker Pam had
just put a plate of sausage sandwiches on the table among
the cards and matches, when the bell rang twice and
Dickey came up the stairs with two big Pipkin cans of
beer. Pam, Joyce and Lenny gave him more than his
usual non-existent welcome and his coat was taken, the
beer was taken and glasses were taken from the bar and
filled before he sat down. Sidonie knew she would have

to drink two glasses before she could talk to him, but she had seen in the inside pocket of his old navy blue overcoat a tall bottle screwed in tissue paper. The television sound was loud so no one heard a child crying upstairs and Lenny secretly refilled Sidonie's glass, so that she was terrified that Pam might pause in her knitting and see.

'What are you knitting, Pam?'

'A school pullover for Nicholas. Poor little sod's got both his elbows coming through.'

'How's old Dickey then?' asked Lenny after half an hour, in a commercial.

'Living,' said Dickey, making a mistake because the Beacons were momentarily united in sorting out his problems and forcing disastrous advice on him. As a diversion he produced the whisky from his coat but as they drank his whisky they rearranged and ruined his life. His girl friend was mocked, his rent exorbitant, his job ill paid, his leisure a bore. Lenny sat back a white froth on his lip and his outstretched legs absorbing all the heat from the fire. Pam sat forward in her chair, wearing a white cardigan, her bare legs slightly apart, her nails clicking against her glass. Joyce was already giggling. The bell rang again – it was George, Sidonie's cousin and a friend. They came into the room rubbing their hands and blowing on them, the friend diffidently and George obscuring the fire. Their faces were red and watery from riding a scooter in the wind and gradually faded as they pushed their unhelmeted hair into place.

Sidonie was glad to see George, a representative from the outside world; he sat beside her, talking about her family and proving to the Beacons she had an existence. He accepted the beer Lenny forced on him, lifting it occasionally from the floor and sipping it like mouthwash. Lenny secretly filled and refilled her glass while George spoke of family, friends and gardens. Dickey was telling Pam about the Air Force in the war, he was a deserter, and Joyce was dancing with Lenny. Sidonie had always used George's marriage as a criterion. Their flat was full of undisplayed photographs of Margaret who, now pregnant for the second time, waited for George at home, happy without alcohol. George went up to the bathroom and then Sidonie, moving on to his warm cushion, remembered a poster for the Scotsman and the words floated about in her mind – An island of sanity in a sea of hysteria; a little black island in wavy red lines. George was the only one who could save her from the Beacons. When he came out she was waiting by the bathroom door.

'George, I want to talk to you. There's something I

want to tell you – no listen,' catching his arm, 'no, listen George – ' Someone was coming up the stairs. She dropped his arm and turned to walk down the stairs passing Pam, who seemed in a hurry, with the top five buttons of her cardigan undone. At the foot of the stairs Sidonie turned and whispered:

'When I go upstairs follow me.'

'What?'

'Follow me when I go upstairs.'

They sat down; she watched his arms accept a cigarette, lift a glass, in the neat suit of an inhabitant of the island of sanity. Pam had come back and taken off her cardigan, her hair falling forward on either side of her neck above the flames as she bent over the fireguard to poke the fire. On the screen grey figures faded into the Stork Margarine commercial; Pam stretched out a creamy arm and turned the sound down and began talking to Dickey, her mouth in profile opening and closing like the terrible dry clack-clack of a stork's beak. Sidonie looked away and wondered what the time was and walked stiffly on unco-ordinated legs to the door and closed it behind her. She used her hands on the more difficult stairs. After a bit George came up and asked her what was the matter but she had forgotten and knew only that he was her salvation.

'Oh yeah, George. I've got something to tell you only you must promise not to tell anyone. OK? Promise?'

He averted his face and pulled away his sleeve.

'Yes, yes, I promise. What is it?'

'Not even Margaret. OK? I mean I know she's your wife and all and you probably tell her everything but don't tell her this. OK?'

'I've promised six times. We've been standing on these cold stairs for thirteen minutes. What do you want to tell me?'

'Listen, George, I'm being driven insane – they – '

Lenny's voice shouted upstairs, 'What are you two doing up there?'

She ran downstairs looking back into George's face with a sob which he interpreted as a giggle. Lenny searched their faces for traces of lipstick, flushes or wet lips.

Then George and his friend were standing up in coats and buckling on crash helmets and she was seized by a fit of humiliating hiccups.

'I'll see you to the door.'

'It's all right, I'll go,' said Lenny, his body in the doorway.

Pam, her white cardigan trailing, was emptying an

ashtray into the ashes of the fire and organizing dirty glasses.

When they got up, it was still Saturday and Sidonie was invited into the kitchen for coffee. It was warm, the clock said five to twelve, and the children's voices came inoffensively from another room. She put her hands round the pink mug and watched her cigarette burning in the ashtray. Then Pam and Lenny moved into action in their invincible partnership, Pam fetching the crying baby and replacing the smell of coffee with the steamy odour of powder, and Lenny, replacing the cigarette in his mouth with a stream of hot coffee, said, 'Old Cousin George fancies you, doesn't he?'

'What do you mean?'

His fingers danced like girls' thighs on the table.

'It's pretty obvious from the way he looked at you.'

'For Christ's sake he's my cousin.'

'Why did he follow you upstairs then?'

'Even Dickey remarked on it,' said Pam.

'It's not true. We were just talking.' She had to shout above the baby's crying and would have liked to sweep it off the table with her hand.

'Don't get so upset, dear. It's quite usual for these things to happen in families.

'Has he ever made a pass at you?'

'Never.'

'What were you doing in the bathroom together for half an hour? Pam says you looked pretty guilty when she came up.'

'Don't get so upset. Why don't you just admit it?'

'I'm not getting upset.' And she had to gulp the hot coffee and get to the draining board quickly before they drowned the island of sanity in the sea of hysteria.

She stood in front of the triple mirror and three pale faces stared back above their dark denim dresses, altering their eyes, three hands pushing back dark hair. Although late, she didn't want to go into the kitchen to say good-bye. She opened the window and picked up a dead fly from the window-sill by its bent black eyelash legs and dropped it into the thick air, leaving a wing that stuck to a tea stain in the dust. Then she combed her hair again, the comb pink with black interstices, her hands yellowish in the light.

Four pairs of identical brown eyes round the table, and Pam's and Lenny's darker and lighter at each end, stared as she came into the doorway.

'I'm going now. Good-bye.'

Lenny said, 'It's a pity you have to go to your Mum's.

We're all going for a walk this afternoon. Ring her up and tell her you can't come.'

'No, I can't.' Her hand was sweating on the doorknob. Above the sound of knives and forks crashing in gravy and 'Sidonie's stupid, she doesn't want any lunch.' 'She going to her mummy's.' 'Why does everybody have to have more than me?' 'Shut your mouth.' 'Shut mouf,' Lenny said. 'Go on, I'll ring her and tell her you're not well.'

'No, I've got to go now I'm late. Good-bye.'

By the time she got to Penge and was walking past people cleaning cars, and Sunday afternoon music playing from an open window over barren hydrangeas, and was met by her father's Pekingese, she half existed again.

'Pam was very upset you wouldn't come out with us this afternoon,' whispered Lenny when she got home.

There was a letter from Lewis among the bills next morning.

Between the glass and the mouth was always his face and now it was above the blue shirt at Charing Cross. He was already under the clock, the evening paper folded at the sports page in his pocket, and she felt an immovable smile stretching her mouth as she walked all the way across the booking-hall and walked up to him, looking not into his eyes but at his smile, which was also fixed.

'On time for once.'

When he said, 'Where would you like to go?' the words which had so often made her stiff with hate made her want to hold his hand.

'I don't know. Let's have a coffee somewhere first while we decide.'

They sat on stools opposite a mirror, her face in the yellow light less lovely than of late, eyes shadowed by drowning, not remembering. On the dark steps of the News Theatre they followed the torch with his kiss still wet on her mouth. He took her hand, but when she offered him one of the peppermint creams she had chosen in the foyer he refused and she remembered he hated them. She wished they could stay for ever in the dark with the coloured screen in front of their eyes, without the risk of words. After seeing the programme one and a half times he wanted to leave and she stood up immediately, wondering if she had been like this when she first knew him. They went to St James's Park, quietly walking by the lake, Sidonie afraid to speak with soiled lips.

'You'll have to give up drinking and smoking. We'll have to save if we're going to get married.'

'I don't mind.'

They sat on a bench by the lake watching birds on the darkening water as railings and bushes faded and sometimes feet were heard on the gravel. In the dark of the park cigarettes glowed as she remembered him among the oleanders and flying ducks and knew that if this time they failed there would come the pain not gin not tears could ameliorate.

The next day Pam gave her an ultimatum.

'I'm giving you an ultimatum. Him or me.'

'You've got Lenny.'

'That's different. I don't want to sit at home thinking of that creep pawing you about.'

'What do you think it's like for me at night?'

'You knew I was married. Anyway, there's not much to be jealous of these days.'

She would have to persuade Joyce to move with her, go to an employment bureau, live at Beacons' till they left. Although her shorthand speed was good and the prospect of normal life attracted, she had not the strength and Pam was still sometimes nice.

'I have written to Lewis.'

'Good girl.'

After waking and refusing to wake several times in the night and after it was morning, she finally opened her

eyes, thinking it was late because the light behind the
closed curtains seemed of the afternoon, and was disappointed to find it was only 11.55. An envelope lay
caught in the broken lino half under the door and she
lay looking at it for five minutes before she dared go and
pick it up. Her feet were cold on the warm Axminster,
and it was not until she had been back in bed for several
minutes that she pulled the letter from beneath the warm
blankets and tore it open above the familiar writing
that was already a wound. She read it calmly and the
words sank below the surface of her mind to join all the
other words, blows, letters that made her wake up in
the morning wondering why.

There was a knock on the door and Pam came in with
a plate and mug and pulled back the curtains and let in
the light from the grey water that obscured and fell
past the window.

'Who was your letter from?'

She put the plate down beside the bed, the red juice of
tomatoes running into the yellow of the round crusty
toast and seeds swimming in butter.

'Lewis.'

'Can I see it?' which was really a statement.

'It's not interesting. You don't want to see it.'

Pam sat down on the bed.

'No more secrets, no more lies, remember?'

'Yes, but there's nothing in this letter, it's not even interesting; in fact it's one of the least interesting letters I've ever read. I wouldn't like you to inflict the boredom of it on yourself.'

The brown and white eyes were looking at her, the white hand poised. She gave her the letter but snatched it back.

'Look, I gave him up for you, isn't that enough?'

'I'll be in to see if you want more tea.'

Sidonie's hands shook as she slopped hot tea on to the sheet and into her mouth. The beautiful tomatoes tasted cold and salty; she wrapped the last ring round a soggy crust and wiped it round the plate. Pam had been gone five minutes. She grabbed the letter from under the pillow and tore it across diagonally and vertically into tiny pieces and shoved them under the pillow so that some fell over the edge of the mattress. Someone knocked on the door and Lenny, not Pam, came in and stood in the corner of the box that contained them both.

'You know what you promised Pam.'

She pulled the covers over her head to annihilate by ignoring him but he pulled them off. In the cold light his face was opaque, bones defined by flesh and brown congealed eyes firm in the thick surface.

'. . . give it to me, dear.'

His words dissolved in the grey light, separating them.

'I've torn it up.' When she told Lenny the truth she wanted to retract it, but the evidence was there in retractable ballpoint and she lifted her hand and a scrap of paper fell to the floor.

'Darlin', you shouldn't have done it. Pam's goin' to be furious.'

'It's my letter.'

'Don't be childish.' He picked up the dishes and went out, shaking his hair. She wondered whether to get dressed, so as to be less vulnerable, but as half dressed was more so, she lay on her stomach to stifle the heartbeats, waiting for the door to click, which it did, and not turning round, felt Pam's heels shake the floor.

'Well?'

She turned and saw the pale blue housecoat open, white legs slightly knotted at the knees. The gas fire exploded out. She feared the stained housecoat hanging drably above white legs, the ringed hands, the stomach that had borne the stain of her kiss a slight swelling beneath pale nylon, and the polished skin of the waiting face with hard cheekbones and her hair behind her ears.

'Give it to me.'

She shook her head as her voice must necessarily sound ridiculous.

'You'll be sorry if I have to take it.'

Sidonie pulled up the pillow and gathered up a pile of fragments and Pam filtered them through her fist.

'Where's the rest?'

'Perhaps some fell down the back.' She bent down and picked up a little heap of insults and dust from beneath her bed and handed them to her.

'And you can take that stupid grin off your face.'

She started laughing as Pam put the dust in her pocket with dignity, and didn't stop when she slapped her face and slammed the door. The scraps were placed in an envelope on the top shelf of the kitchen cupboard and never pieced together.

She took the Underground to Holborn and walked until she came to the new library. She went down the steps and through a glass door into the reading-room. Her heels clicked loudly on the floor and people looked up from the pale wood tables like members of a club. She took two magazines and sat down opposite a big Nigerian student in a college scarf and found she had chosen *Yachting Monthly* and *Housewife*. To the right was a row of cushioned seats, grey heads bent among bright magazines and old hands shaking the morning papers. An old man, his head tossing in flesh and the pinned lapels of his overcoat, slept; the bare skin between buttons showing a line of dried blood where another pin had been. The room shook with his snores so the woman beside him shook him and eventually an assistant from upstairs came down and warned him. Sidonie wanted to put her head on the desk and sleep but feared to wake to a policeman's touch on her shoulder.

What seemed a young man in a white raincoat, but at the third glance and meeting of his eyes, lines appeared on his face and the raincoat became a tattered beige not less than a decade younger than his thirty-five-year-old face, was sitting across the room from her. The hands on the electric clock pointed to eleven and his eyes were focused on her face.

Sidonie replaced her magazines and left; she thought he would follow her, but when she emerged from the side exit into the snow he was not behind her. She went to the Air Terminal where Lenny waited in the entrance, being avoided by taxis, his nose and hands blue. He removed her hand from hers and placed it in his pocket.

'Where do you want to go, darlin'?'

'I don't know. Anywhere. For a drink.'

'I'm afraid I'm broke, darlin'. I had to give Pam the family allowance. I've got just about enough for a beer each.'

'Let's go anyway. It's freezing.'

In the brown pub, whose only other customer was a purple-faced lady in a fur coat, sitting by the electric fire with her lonely glass of Guinness, Lenny came back from the bar with one large gin in his hand. Lacking the strength to reproach or the grace to thank him, Sidonie drank it at one gulp and walked out of the pub.

The day ended, after the wet screaming of the children in the bath and the white light had receded into the television, with the sound of a glass breaking and Pam Beacon sobbing on the stairs.

The rain turned to sleet next morning as Pam, gulping hot tea through a cracked lip, carrying Lenny's tea downstairs in a pink mug, passed her on the stairs and said good-bye. All the way on the Underground she thought about Pam; Pam crying, Pam bleeding, and on the walk to the library, of Pam taking the children to school, late, running, her eyes red and her swollen lip throbbing in the frozen air, and wished again she had never seen the Beacons.

In the library, grey lumps of snow melted by people's feet and ran out from under their shoes. Sidonie felt her

feet thaw and started to write a letter but couldn't think
of anything to say. Lenny was stuffing fried tomato into
a sullen mouth, his own or Royston's and laying the
knife and fork neatly on the plate and the plate on the
draining board for Pam's frozen fingers to wash when
she got in. From where she sat she could see the man in
the mac looking at her. He had just come in and his face
was grey, the pores contracted round the stubble on his
chin. He sat with his hands in his armpits. Across the
table from her sat a man, the top of his head covered with
a grey dressing held to the bald freckled surface by
strips of scarcely adhering white elastoplast, so that he
looked like an egg someone had started to eat but found
distasteful. He coughed and wiped something off the
newspaper.

Sidonie bent over her letter.

'Dear' – twenty to eleven by the electric clock.

The word stood stupidly on the blue page, a greeting
to someone not dear and also cheap, and was 'Dear' the
customary form of address, or would the recipient be
overcome by embarrassment? The second hand moved
round the clock-face, ticking her life away and the lives
of the others surrounded and silhouetted by silence as
snow fell outside.

The man came over and stood beside her table. He

spoke; he was a Scot and deaf in one ear, so had to bend over her.

'Do you like reading?'

'Yes.'

'Do you like poetry?'

'Yes.'

'I thought you might. I've some poetry here I might show you.'

He took from his inside jacket pocket a little red note-book, several folded envelopes, and a passport joined together with an elastic band and put them on the table. He handed her a piece of paper from the notebook and took it back, saying, 'I've a better version here some-where,' and after five minutes gave it to her.

> When the traffic lights are red
> I'll remember you are dead.
> When the traffic lights are amber
> It's your hair that I'll remember.
> When the traffic lights are green
> I'll remember you Maureen.

'It's very nice.'

'This one's like Stockhausen. You know Stock-hausen? It's like fragments of piano music set out on a chart and you play any fragment at random and the tempo mark at the end of it shows you the tempo for the next random choice. Get it?'

Final Parting

After the last issue
You sneeze – reach for a tissue.
It's over. I'll miss you,
The cancer that is you.
Have someone to kiss you
When your subscription is due
And ask God to bless you.

That's you. It's over,
Is due, after the last
To bless you, you sneeze.
To kiss you have someone
Issue when your subscription
I'll miss you.
Reach for a tissue, the cancer.

After the last – I'll miss you
You sneeze – (to) bless you
It's over – reach for a tissue
The cancer – is due
Have someone – issue
When your subscription – that is you
And ask God to kiss you.

'Then there's this unfinished poem about primroses, I think that's an interesting subject – I don't see many poems about primroses, do you?'

'No. What's this mean, "Macmillan at the Virginals"?'

'That's an idea I had for a cartoon. You know that picture in the National Gallery, Girl at the Virginals? Well, I thought Macmillan at the Virginals. It's just an idea.'

'Don't touch that,' he said closing the cover quickly on a woman's face stern from the joint passport.

'I must go now. I've got to meet someone,' said Sidonie into his cupped ear, and repeated it.

'I'm going myself. You go first and I'll meet you outside. No one must see us leave together.'

When she stood outside in the snow she wanted to run, thinking at all cost she must escape human contact, but he came out of the side exit too and started walking down the little back street into perhaps Grays Inn Road.

'What do you do with yourself?'

'What do you do with yourself?' It seemed slightly funny; he didn't hear her.

'Are you an art student?'

'Yes.'

'Where?'

'St Martin's.'

'Are you on holiday, or what?'

'No. I just didn't feel like going in today.'

'What date did the term commence?' with the typical Scots preoccupation with terms, exam results, academic qualifications.

'Oh God – I don't know,' she tried to say casually, her hands clenching on the crumbs in her pockets with panic – once the glib liar.

'When did you say?'

'I don't remember. I'm not a walking calender,' She suddenly knew he had connections and had recognized the deceit from the start.

'What year are you in?'

'Second.'

'Second?'

As a little diversion she picked up a handful of grey snow from a ledge and threw it at him, but it was ill received by the shabby face and she felt she was a secret vagrant, sleeping on the embankment but ashamed to admit it and unworthy of the others in the library, and he knew it.

'Did you see that lady to your left in the library?'

'The one with long grey hair, (stockings rolled round her ankles, arm in a dirty sling)?'

'The one in the grey coat?'

'Yes. Why?'

'She works as a model at St Martin's sometimes.'

'Oh. I thought I'd seen her somewhere.'

'She hasn't worked there for three years.'

They came to a road intersection and on the crossing he took her arm to pull her back from the silver wheels of an E-type Jaguar. Sidonie guessed he had not even a furnished room, and wondered what he thought when he saw cars and supermarkets and televisions and cinemas; especially at Christmas, walking past lit windows at 2 a.m. displaying cards, anomalous gifts, bath salts, talc, food and the whole entertainment world of which he had no part.

'Is this the way to Holborn?'

'What do you want at Holborn?'

'I have to meet someone there at twelve – I wonder what the time is?' There was a clock outside a shuttered jewellers.

'It's only about eleven-thirty. Don't worry, I'll get you to Holborn on time. Is it your boy friend you're meeting?'

'Just a friend.'

Checking with consecutive clocks they passed, she assessed the time as ten to twelve.

'Time for a cup of tea.'

They stopped at a café door, he half entered, the waitress shook her head, and he turned.

'Not this place. It's not very clean.'

In the café they went to, she sat while he went to the counter and came back with two teas and two three-penny Kit-Kats in the saucers. He sat opposite her, his black stringy tie dividing unequally the dirty white shirt which bore burns, sick, ketchup, ash, the marks of all the atrocities which can happen to a shirt when it's your only one. The chocolate was melting against the side of the cup and on her fingers as she broke it and forced it in four sections into her starving mouth. He took from his pocket, tangled with a handkerchief, an empty five Weights packet which he crushed and put in the ashtray and after talk, unheard on one side, unlistened to on the other, they went out to a sky of peach and inclement weather. Wind and blown rain across the pavements and scattered showers from the sides of shops, bright angles of glass suddenly blurred. His mac blew open from its button and he held it down with his hands in his pockets and she smiled at him.

'Where are we going?'

'To the Wall of Death.'

'The Wall of Death?'

She couldn't think what it was, although the name was familiar – three prisoners against a wall at dawn or twenty-five past three in the afternoon, the volley, crumpled fall. Then she remembered black and grey newspaper pictures of the motorcyclist on the sheer wall, the caption, then crushed spokes, a blanket.

They had come to a little gate in a wall which he held open for her and she went in. It was a grey square with iron seats and in the flower beds under dark green bushes a few drab birds pecked. He walked in front of her to a seat on which he sat and said, 'Shall we sit down a minute?'

To their right was the back of a brick building with smoking chimneys. He pointed: 'The Wall of Death.' Tombstones were incorporated in the walls of the square and paving stones underfoot, half names, half sentiments corroded by soot. It was quiet and Sidonie had to make an effort against her sense of inevitability. She let him take her hand.

'What is this place?'

The garden of St John? Mary? Paul? She didn't hear.

'I like holding your hand.'

'Do you?' She let it stay with his but didn't return the squeeze, wondering is there a hair in my gum, no it's only my palate feels soft through so much chewing. His

face with the scent of hyacinths was turned from her
and she asked, 'Before you came to London what did
you do?'

'I'm a chemist – research.'

'Must be very interesting.'

'Well, yes and no. I suppose to the layman it seems so.
No, as I was saying in the café, beware the Bohemian
life. You're young.'

'Why?' She was aloof from his answer, watching
black birds flying in the white sky. When she forced her
thoughts back: ' – Edinburgh. I did this big painting of a
ballet dancer on raw canvas. It was about ten feet by
twelve feet. It was really beautiful though I say it myself,
her skirt all white and arabesque and that, and the background dark green. Anyway, I had to go away to
hospital for two or three weeks and when I came back
the landlady had used it to mend the roof.'

'How terrible for you,' and he pulled her face to his
and kissed her, his breath smelling of hyacinths or
carnations. After what she judged to be a decent interval
of a few seconds, she withdrew her mouth and giving
the false smile which did not fail to charm, stood up,
fighting her feeling of timelessness and his timelessness,
but he pulled her down and holding her hand in his
pocket said:

'You're a very warm person.'

'Oh,' inconsequential little laugh; 'well, I've really got to go now,' and after a few kisses, as he walked her through unfamiliar streets, she was planning how to make it seem as though she was a warm person from whom he was separated by circumstance. As they stood outside Holborn tube station, she accidentally bit the side of her mouth, so that the grey gum was dyed red and, rejecting it, she agreed to meet him the next day at the library, and watched his mac disappear through the tiled archway before walking past the ticket collector on to the downward escalator.

She and Lenny sat in a pub till ten past three, then walked in the warmer air till five and she met Joyce in the road and they went in together, but Joyce went out again. Lenny went to work and Sidonie watched television; Pam had a bath and came down scented into the silence.

Wednesday morning broke in the kitchen with streaks of watery sun shining as on destruction after days of famine and flood. Blue and yellow flames roared under the percolator's chrome and dusty glass. A long pool of water on the table drowned the blue roses and when the wind blew water spattered the window and the light blew from the cool and fragile eggs in the bowl.

Long shells lay about the table; alone, gleaming inside, the tough white circle at the base unbroken; or white half jammed into brown and shattering. Beneath the window, Earls Court Station lay like roofs of houses showing above the flood; the platforms were grey sheets of water and a man working on the rails looked up into the blown grey sky, the sun reflecting on his pick.

In the changing light across the window shapes changed; knives dulled and shone, dust danced in a stream to the brown lino, shadows fell from cups, egg-shells, hands, then joined the shadows on the walls. The gas flames burned fiercely when the windows blurred and cold in the sun. At the stove, Lenny put on to a plate, wings, brain, eyes, beak and legs in one white and golden protein circle, sunny side up, which was followed into his mouth by a piece of toast called a finger. Bowls on the table showed the metamorphosis of Weetabix; crisp against the blue china, soggy with added milk and heaped sugar crystals, then a hard brown cement round the edges of the bowl and spoon, which hot and cold water beating into the polythene basin could not remove without detergent and hands.

Before Sidonie reached the library the door swung open and he stood on the steps, his mac blown against the momentarily gold glass door; he looked down the road away from her and then walked towards her holding his mac together with his hands in his pockets.

'I was just giving you up.'

'Yes, well, it's a wonder I got here at all. I just came to tell you I've got to go to Wales for a month.'

'Wales?'

'Yes, my uncle just died and I've got to go up for the funeral and then stay and help my aunt on the farm for a bit.'

They were walking along, his ear bent to her.

'Has your auntie a farm?'

'Yes. I just came to tell you. I have to go immediately, I've got to meet my brother at Euston at eleven.'

'Come and have a cup of tea first. Where have you got to get to?'

'Euston. I haven't time, really. I'd love to, but my brother's got all my luggage.'

They passed a café and he stopped.

'Just come in and sit down a minute. I've something to say to you.'

She hesitated, he pushed the door and they went in, but the girl behind the counter shook her head at him and he pulled the door open and they went out again.

'That woman owes me money and she's ashamed to

meet me.' He didn't speak the rest of the way to the station but in the booking-hall said:

'I'll not come any further. Your brother might not like it. Will I see you again?'

'Yes, if you want to. Have you an address or anything I could write to? Where do you live?'

'I live in a hostel in Old Street. It's not a nice place. I wouldn't like you to see it.'

'What's it like then?'

'It is so – demoralizing. I've all my books and documents in a locker at Charing Cross, but I can't afford to get them out. Mind, I've a friend in Guernsey who can get me a job any time; in fact, I may go over there later in the year.'

She said, 'Excuse me a minute, please,' and went over to the shop and bought ten Weights. He wouldn't take them at first, then she said, 'Please I want you to have them. Anyway I don't smoke much,' and he took them and offered her one, which she accepted, and he struck a light from one of the two matches in his box and lit it for her.

'I've something for you, too. It's not much, but I hope you'll accept it. I use it myself sometimes, not because I'm effeminate, mind, but I like to keep myself nice.' It was a little half-empty bottle of carnation perfume with a pink screw cap and when she opened it she smelled his coat, his hair, his breath.

Lenny and Sidonie spent the afternoon in the Air Terminal and he ordered soup and until it came insisted that croutons were croissants. They sat immobile in deep leather chairs, while flights were called and their companions disappeared and returned with different faces and luggage.

'Can't get any more cigarettes on tick, darlin'.' Sidonie did not reply because she had been informed two days ago that Lenny had arranged for the tobacconist to refuse Pam credit.

Lenny had not spoken to Pam for a week; his meals congealed on the table or cracked in the oven and Pam developed a stye. She told Joyce he came into the bedroom shouting 'Wake up' and pulled the covers off and punched her in the face. 'So I thought I might as well lie back and enjoy it.' Joyce repeated this to Sidonie, who, when she accused Lenny, outraged him into shocked denial and left him standing by the station entrance. She had made arrangements to see a friend she had met in the street, but instead walked for hours through the fog.

She came up the cold stairs that smelled of onions and fog drifted up to the first floor and the squeaking door where her hand hesitated before turning the handle and surprise surprise Lenny was standing on a chair, laughing, with the light reflecting on his head and three glasses in his hands, and Joyce was dancing with a tall Indian, and there were faceless shapes on the sofa because her eyes went first to the record player where the beautiful disc jockey, goddess of music in Lenny's socks, stood swaying, an L.P. clasped to her, her feet and the music not coinciding. Lenny said: 'Sidonie this is – and – and – '

'And this is my beautiful darling and she's smiling at me.'

'Pour yourself a drink.' There was a bottle of whisky, a quarter gone, and another lay on its side, the last drop leaking round its mouth.

'Don't take too much,' shouted Pam, through red lips stretched and distended in an inverted glass.

Lenny poured another drink into Sidonie's half empty tumbler and when she began to feel detached, she went and started talking to one of the men on the sofa. Pam was dancing with Lenny.

'You look sad.'

'No.'

He pulled her hands and asked her to dance.

'No, I don't want to dance.'

'Everyone wants to dance. It's a basic emotion.'

'No.'

She lifted his wrist, where silver and luminous among dark hairs, his watch lay, and saw it was nearly two. She looked at Pam. She was sitting across a chair and only her legs showed; her feet swung in Lenny's socks up to the golden calf, socks where his feet had sweated that symbolized more than a ring the blundered bond. Sidonie jumped up, kicking over a glass and not retrieving it. She bent over the chair and said:

'Pam I want to talk to you.'

'Go ahead – talk.'

'No, listen, Pam, I want to talk to you. I've got something interesting to tell you in the kitchen. Come on.' She pulled her by the hands and her feet crashed to the floor. Pam stood up, the shock of her feet transmitted to her blank eyes, and pushing her upstairs in front of her, Sidonie rested her fist in the small of the back she had not touched for so long. She slammed the kitchen door and pulled her into her arms and kissed her hard on the mouth, pressing her against herself until she heard her shoulders crack. Then the woman she had been going to kill, for whom her hand groped towards the knife-and-fork drawer, began to kiss her back, and this time tears fell from her eyes and poured down her face in a stream of incoherence and lipstick. Pamela.

'Let's go into the bedroom,' said Pam, and in the cold

room on the un-made bed, Pam's sweat on her face, locked in the arms of her lover, she tried to kid herself she would love her for ever.

After Pam had gone downstairs, she lay for a few minutes staring at the ceiling, where fog drifted through the closed windows and in wisps round the yellow light-bulb. Then she washed her face in cold water in the kitchen, went past a boy standing in the bathroom with the door open, and downstairs, two at a time.

Lenny was trying to find Luxemburg on the wireless and the room was filled with distortion as the bright needle swung through the jewelled stations of Kalunborg, Prague, Hilversum. Pam was not there. She lay flaked out, face downwards on her bed, and Lenny and the party proceeded without her.

In the morning, freezing fog hung behind the closed curtains like storm windows and Sidonie woke from a dream to the alarm clock and a song in her head.

> So here hath been dawning
> Another blue day.
> Think, wilt thou let it
> Slip useless away?

and put on a record to drown it, and struck a match to light the fire. There was no gas. The children were playing barefoot in pyjamas, three of them in the bedroom and one crying in the kitchen.

'Royston, Royston, do you want a Smartie?' Crash! as the door slammed in his face.

'Royston, Royston, the door's open, come on. Don't you want any Smarties?' Thump. Crash.

Joyce, provider of breakfast, shoved half a crown in the meter on her way out past the bedroom where ex-breadwinner Beacon, his scalp cold among the flared hair, pulled the sheet over his head and wondered whether to pretend to be asleep or to shout for his tea.

Upstairs in front of the kitchen mirror Pam tried to smear the last pink smudges of Max Factor Candleglow out of the jar and over three long scratches on her neck.

Not wanting to see her, Sidonie went straight out without stopping to borrow the toothpaste and, her mouth feeling like a stable, from the night before, bought some chewing gum at the station for sixpence. They had none for twopence-halfpenny and in consequence she had a halfpenny left in her pocket and had to wait for Lenny in a phone booth, holding the empty receiver to her ear, as she did so often that winter in so many phone booths, and tried to tell herself there was nothing unnatural in waiting there for a man she hated, the sodden yellow cover of A–D on the floor, NIGS on the wall, a man making kissing noises through the window, his breath leaving cold smudges on the dirty window, and always expecting Pam's distorted face, accusing.

'Lenny will be a bit late today.'

'Lenny?'

'Come off it. I know you're waiting for him. You might as well come home.'

'Home!'

When Lenny came, first pointed feet with trousers growing out of them, then the check coat, and at the foot of the steps, the smiling face, Lenny in entirety, she could not bring herself to speak to him.

'Where do you want to go? Where, darlin'?'

After four minutes had passed on the station clock, with Lenny's mouth and voice gesturing at her as if through soundproof glass, he walked through the barrier without buying tickets and she followed him into the lift.

'I wish you'd stop chewin' in that adolescent way.'

'Got a hangover?'

'What have I done to make you stop speakin' to me?'

'Don't credit yourself with the power to stop me speaking.'

In the SKR restaurant at South Kensington the unasked for tomato soup grew cold on the table as Sidonie, although starving, played with the roll on her plate.

'Please eat something, darlin'.'

'Very well. I was just waiting for you to say it ten times. That was nine.'

'Please eat something.'

'Darlin'.'

'Please eat something, darlin'.'

She took out her chewing gum and wrapped it in a piece of paper and handed it to him.

'Put that in your pocket, please' and as he took it, 'Be careful not to touch it.'

Hating herself as much as him, she tried to add some heat to the soup with pepper; herself less, on reflection, remembering the secret blows in the night, empty meters, her tears, and Pam's on different storeys far into the night.

'I had a surprise planned for you today.'

'But I'm not going to get it, as I've been so horrible.'

'It's not something you can get.'

'What is it? Please tell me, look, I'm being all nice.'

A surprise – a vision of a parcel in Christmas paper and ribbon had flashed into her head, but she wasn't really excited and could have watched diamonds float down the gutter.

'Please, Lenny darling.'

He opened his clenched fist and a key lay shining on the table among spilt salt and stains.

'What is it?'

'Take it, it's yours.'

He was smiling all over his face, then he sneezed and said from behind a handkerchief:

'Go on – take it.'

It lay cold and ominous in her hand, a Yale.

'What's it for?'

'To open a door. Our door. I've found a place where we can go. Just think, darlin', no more snow, no more Air Terminal, a place of our own.'

She looked down at the key, where it lay blurred and doubled, the final key to lock her to him. She saw herself crash through the window and run, the key thrown over her shoulder, bleeding, free, anywhere away from him, but in the metropolis, the Underground, the sky, there was nowhere to go. She looked up and saw his eyes filled with pleading and disappointment. Then he sneezed again and wiped his nose defeatedly, also his eyes.

'I thought you'd be pleased.'

She managed to smile and say through unfalling tears:

'Of course I am, only it's so unexpected.' And victorious again, he put away his weapons, handkerchief, tears, voice.

'Do you want to see it now?'

'Yes.'

The room in Notting Hill was filled with the scent of roses and water dripped through the ceiling. Sidonie turned and saw her face in a long mirror with the word 'Roses!' on her lips.

'Yes, darlin'. I'm going' to have the ceiling fixed tomorrow – I could probably do it myself.'

'It doesn't matter.'

She wondered what he would have done with the roses if she hadn't come. Left them to die, or carried his floral humiliation down to the dustbin, or laid them with a snarl on the kitchen table – 'Here you are, cow!'

She picked up a green bottle that stood among fallen petals and played with the silver cap.

'Who does it belong to?'

'You, darlin'.'

'No, who owns it I mean?'

'You.'

'Who do you rent it from?'

'Never mind, darlin'. Do you want a drink?' He

poured the gin into the cup. On the shelf was a packet of assorted biscuits. 'Sit down.'

There was only the bed to sit on. The room was small and from the window she could see seagulls flying round the top of the Mac Fisheries building.

Lenny, his fingers rustling the wrapper, a custard cream half in his mouth said, 'Try one of these biscuits, darlin', they're delicious. Why not?'

'I hate biscuits. I don't really – I'm not hungry.'

He had the perfect mouth for assorted biscuits and a pink wafer followed, failing to dislodge a custard cream from the corner of his mouth. There was a record player on the floor by the gas ring and 'When I Grow Too Old to Dream' by Gracie Fields on 78.

'I'll have to get some decent records for you.'

'So what's indecent about Gracie Fields? Anyway, I've got lots of records.' She put the record on and refilled her cup. Lenny sat on the floor leaning against the bed, his head poised for stroking. Sidonie held her cup in both hands, while moving his arm with her foot to see that it was eleven o'clock. She put the record on again.

> We had been gay
> Going our way.
> Life had been beautiful

We had been young.
After you've gone
Life will go on
Like an old song that is sung.

So kiss me, my sweet,
And so let us part,
And when I grow too old to dream,
That kiss will stay in my heart.

Her cup was empty, the song made her cry. It started the third time and they settled down to domesticity, with gin and tears and dripping water and Lenny mimicking in a high falsetto:

When I grow too old to dream,
I'll have you to remember.
And when I grow too old to dream,
Your love will live in my heart.

and Lenny trampling through books and records and people, spoiling, spoiling, spoiling.

'Darlin'.' A few days later Sidonie lay on the bed while Lenny, his face inflamed from the gas ring, heated some condensed mushroom soup. He had a pedantic way of doing this which involved slowly pouring the water, a few drops at a time, from the empty tin into the mushroom soup, meanwhile stirring until each drop was assimilated. Despite this the cooked soup was as badly integrated as Pam's, who emptied contents, added water, boiled.

'I've arranged to stay here tonight.'

'Why?'

'Just think, darlin', a whole night together. I've never had a night alone with you. Don't look so upset. I won't do anything you don't want me to.'

'I can't stay here.'

She was leaning against the mantelpiece, the muscle in her leg tensed almost to breaking and the casual hand in her hair ripping it slowly from the roots.

'Why not? I've never taken advantage of you, have I, darlin'?'

'We can't both be away the same night.'

'Do not worry. Everythin' is arranged. Beacon has arranged everythin'. I stay here tonight and tomorrow. You stay at your mother's tomorrow, as far as Pam's concerned. See?'

'No.'

'Darlin', don't reject me, I can't bear it. I've so longed to hold you in my arms at night.'

'Well, so long then. I'm going.'

As he jumped to bar the door the soup boiled over

quenching the gas and splashing his shoe. He pushed her to the edge of the bed and sat her down hard with his hands on her shoulders. With each slap across her face, the smell of burnt soup was cut off, returned, cut off, she put her hands over her screaming face and kicked him in the stomach, and groaning and grabbing his groin, he pushed her over and hit her round the head, shoulders, anywhere, until suddenly he dropped to the floor and sobbed.

'You treat me like dirt, you treat me like bloody dirt' with soup and tears on his hands and shirt and trousers and the escaping gas roaring through the ring by his head.

'I wish I was dead,' he wept and turned off the gas.

For a long time after his tears ceased and she had heard him wash and dry his big face and the floor and stove, Sidonie lay face downwards on the bed. His breathing was normal now; she couldn't hear it. She hoped her face was swollen, and touching it with her finger, felt the marks of his fingers. She wondered what Lenny was doing; he was staring at his swollen eyes in the mirror. She heard a match strike and gas ignite; lying as the blind who, waiting helpless for a meal, hear the spoon stirring arsenic, the tin opener rattling against Kit-E-Kat. When he put his hand on her shoulder, she didn't move and when he raised her head it fell backwards, eyes closed and mouth hanging frighteningly open. Still supporting her, his cold fingers scrabbled frantically for her heart and finding it with a sob laid her down on the bed and bathed her face tenderly with the end of a towel dipped in the sink and watered it with his own tears, which stung where they fell and itched. He knelt beside her and the dim pages of a First Aid manual flicking through his mind, he, a tall youth in shorts and long socks, bent on one knee to loosen the clothing of his shocked and shingled love. She sat up, with her sweater half over her head. 'Necrophile'. He clasped his arms round her and laid his head against her so she could see the pores on top of his head and the useless down that grew on his arid scalp. 'I suppose this is a silence too deep for words,' she thought, and remembered a poem she had written, its final line 'A silence too deep for tears' in black on the glossy page of the school magazine; and looking down on Lenny's head, thought of her friend Julie leaning forward on the cloakroom bench to lace a plimsoll and saying, 'I'm going to make men suffer' and who now lived in one room above a chemist's in Dulwich, with a legitimized baby and a husband who didn't like her.

Lenny got up without speaking and went over and started serving the remains of the soup, grabbing the pan just as the grey bubbles reached the rim. Sidonie laughed and wished she hadn't when she saw his shoulders move defeatedly in the blue sweater and put her arm round his shoulder in the gesture that had often been her downfall. He turned with a smile, lips lunging and she, avoiding his kiss, knew it had been a mistake.

While eating without comment the bigger helping she asked:

'What will you do if I don't stay the night to-morrow?'

'Tell Pam you haven't got a job, of course.' Looking at him, his lips pursed savagely to expel carbon dioxide from a stained lung on to a spoonful of soup in order that he might place it in his mouth, she couldn't tell if he meant it.

'You'll have to tell her about you too.'

'She'll forgive me but she won't forgive you.'

Which was why at half past eleven the next morning she was walking round the streets and terraces of Notting Hill and Paddington; Colville, Talbot, Powis. A few dirty icicles hung from the railings round the frozen grass and rotting leaves of locked squares. It was when she stood for the second time, the cold soaking through the soles of her boots, in front of the brick chapel and read that:

The Love of Self is Hell.
The Love of Others Heaven.

and:

Regeneration is that change of Heart and Mind
Which begins when we determine to
Shun Evil and to do Good

that she decided anywhere was better than nowhere and
started to walk towards Lenny. Her head felt empty and
light and the cold was something she walked through,
not felt. The phrase SUICIDE WHILE THE BALANCE OF HIS
MIND WAS DISTURBED kept appearing in her head and the
sign HOSPITAL PLEASE DRIVE QUIETLY – his mind off
balance, the white disc in his head swinging, and the
obituary in the *Kent Messenger*, Dr Kenneth Simpson,
pathologist – a verdict of suicide while the balance of
his mind, lots of people in Penge streets with the
balance of their minds disturbed.

Coroner: '?'

Mrs Martin: 'No. He often used to put his head in the
    oven.'

She read a notice in the window of a closed florist's
shop.

'Dear Friends & Neighbours,
 I should like to thank you all for the kindness
you showed in the event of my husband's death
and for the lovely floral tributes.
                                    Mrs Wadham.

She had been walking round for four hours, her
aching jaws were pumping energy through tasteless
gum, and she felt she could go on for ever. Another
notice, in a butcher's shop – SMART CLEAN LAD WANTED.
A dog clawed at a congealed ball of blood and sawdust,
an entrail dangling from his mouth and his own scraping
the floor through the thin skin.

She shut the door quietly and walked past the table
with its pile of letters to those long since moved,
insurance cards for the dead, telegrams for the non-
existent, up the linoleum staircarpet and when the lino
stopped, the wooden stairs to their room. Lenny sat up
in bed naked, hair rampant on skull beige, raising his
arm, with a smell of sweat, to rub his eyes and push
down his hair.

'What's the time, darlin'?'
'One.'
'One o'clock! Where have you been?'
'I just felt like a walk. Get up, you great slob.'

He snuggled down into the blankets.

'Aren't you going to kiss me?'

'I don't expect so. Get up.'

She went over to the sink, and running the cold tap on her hand, splashed water into his face. Lenny leaped up like a satyr in his sweat, swearing at her. When he spoke, she only nodded or shook her head, wishing to breathe as little of the air as possible. She lit the fire and opened the window, which Lenny, in a vest called a singlet by the label sticking up at the back, closed. Sidonie smoked a cigarette which he lit and she wiped while he went downstairs, and came back to wash in the sink. She made a mental note to use only the edge of the towel.

Now, at 3.20 by their Timecal clock, there was a March sunset shining on the windows of a furniture depository and Victor Sylvester introducing Overseas Requests for Ghana. Lucky Town, Kenya, and it was Adios Muchahas for three inspectors. The sunset had faded before the end of the tango, and when Music While You Work, played by the Band of the Coldstream Guards, conductor Lieutenant Colonel Douglas A. Pope, came on and the signature tune finished Lenny was on top of her, fumbling with buttons and his mouth locked over hers like a wet suction pad with tongue and teeth. She felt removed from him; the air was visible round her. She looked at the door, she couldn't fight him but watched dispassionately as he kissed and sucked at her. Then with terrible inevitability he started to take her clothes off and she, as if through fog, moved to facilitate it and lay stiff as he organized her arms and legs and she suddenly closed her bursting eyes as she took the next passive step in her slow suicide. It didn't last long and then Lenny's head was resting on her and his whole weight pressing on her as he said, 'It'll be better next time, darlin', I promise. It's been so long – ' and his foot in the flabby yellowed nylon sock slid to the floor.

She felt suddenly naked but couldn't get off the bed to get her clothes and had to ask him to hand them to her. She tried to tell herself, 'It wasn't so bad, was it' as if she had been to the dentist, but she knew it was. Beside her on the bed Lenny started to snore and his arm pinned her to the bed. After a few minutes she pushed him off and started to dress while he lay and watched her through sluggish eyes.

Afterwards, she could not remember how they spent the rest of that day, which was a landmark in his life also, except later Lenny went out to the off-licence and she was very sick, perhaps over him.

The milkman refused to deliver. Lenny had not been working – he told Pam he was working in Norfolk, and if she noticed when his and Sidonie's absences coincided, she said nothing. She said little anyway, her mouth was stiff with toothache. So, for the last week Lenny had worked and took money home to Pam. He came into their room, where Sidonie slept, and slept himself until six o'clock – he lay watching her for an hour while she slept, trembling with love for her, the pale jade bracelet on her flung arm, the faint smell of gin on her open lips. He covered her gently and she turned in her sleep on to her stomach and with a little moan pulled the sheet over her and lay with her arms around her head. He got up quietly and poured himself a glass of milk from the carton and as he drank the pure white liquid and watched his lovely one's hands inert above the twisted sheet he thought again how he would love to have a child by her. When she opened her lovely glazed eyes and stared unknowingly round the room, he took her warm body reassuringly in his arms and put her hand where it belonged and kissed her with such love she must have felt it flow into her veins and she opened her eyes wide and pushed him away, the intensity of such love was too much, and holding him, unable to speak, tears came to her eyes. And then they were one again and it was marvellous and it was marvellous for her too. She turned away, beyond words, her hand on his back and the sun lighting up traces of tears or sweat on her face – she woke from the warm blackness and immediately he took her hand, weak as a shelled crab, and put it on him. His tongue invaded her mouth and his teeth knocked on hers. Tears came to her eyes, but did not fall as she performed the double task of making him want to make love to her, but her mouth would not comply when he asked, do you love me? Her throat and hand ached. She looked above his gasping head at the ceiling; the damp had spread round the light fitting and the cold December sun lit a stripe along his back, highlighting a spot.

Light momentarily lace about her legs in the long mirror she dressed and put on the kettle to wash. Cups and saucers were neatly stacked and she knew Lenny had been using the towel to dry the dishes. She fried Lenny an egg, the yolk broke, and Lenny, eating a charred chip of the frying pan, said, 'Delicious omelette, darlin',' He squeezed a new tube of toothpaste and instead of red hexachlorophene rushing to destroy oral bacteria, a pure white strip oozed from a smooth mouth, and he spent the afternoon writing to the manufacturers.

He found a photograph of Lewis while turning out Sidonie's pockets for money for a stamp, and said he had a conceited face and this resulted in a vicious quarrel and Lenny crying:

'I wish I could get you out of my system.'

— your system, lungs deflating and wetly flapping against your ribs, gall bladder, perhaps a little blocked, five-lobed liver gleaming, pulmonary artery pulsating brown blood, and if I bite you, an army of white corpuscles rushing to the rescue.

Sidonie went back to Earls Court to sleep and woke with a sense of futility so great she couldn't open her eyes.

'Fancy meeting you here,' said Joyce. Before she switched from the Home to the Light a voice commanded:

Go sell that thou hast and give to the poor.

'How's Jimmy?'

'Lovely. How's Mike?'

'We may be getting engaged at Christmas.'

They walked into the cold morning. When she got to Notting Hill, there was a long letter from Lenny on the bed of which she read half. The electric fire hummed so loudly in the empty room she had to go out, and groped through jagged tins and paper bags and decaying cheese for some money, weeping at the squalor, while the wastepaper basket stood empty on the floor. When spring came, she felt she would be able to break from Beacon, yet dreaded the first crocus.

As she looked at her reflection among cotton house-frocks, she saw above her head a notice: 'Assistant Wanted'. 'Go and work in D. A. Reeve and give to the poor' she thought sneeringly, but after passing the door twice, went in.

'Excuse me, are you the manageress?' she asked, remembering too late the unstamped insurance card festering in an unknown filing cabinet. The lady, who wasn't the manageress, led her to the manageress and she saw that all the ladies behind the racks of plastic aprons and fully-fashioned stockings wore black and were elderly.

'Good morning. What can I do for you?'

'Good morning. I saw your advertisement in the window.'

'Yes?'

'I would like to apply for the job.'

'Have you had any experience of this type of work as a saleslady?'

'No.'

'Where have you worked before?'

'I was a shorthand typist.'

'When did you leave your last employment?'

'About three – four months ago.'

'I see. Well, I don't really think this job would suit you. We were looking for someone rather older and with more experience.'

She went back by bus, half expecting the conductor to refuse her fare, and washed out a penicillin culture growing in a milk bottle under the sink. When it grew dark she went home, but Pam was in the kitchen so she could get no food. Although for two years she and Joyce had shared clothes and cosmetics, now she couldn't ask her for half a crown.

'What are you doing tonight?'

'Seeing Mike. Why, aren't you doing anything?'

'Yes. I'm going to the 101 later.' And had to because there was nowhere else.

Sidonie my darling,

I'm so far away from you and I feel so dreadfully upset and lonely. Last night I cried myself to sleep because we had had such a lovely day and I wanted the night to be ours as well, but as usual I lost out and I cried with frustration and the aching longing I had for you. I've never longed for 'Death' so much as I did today. Now it seems that the drinking we did together was not really what you wanted but just an escape from my emotions. That I'm neurotic and that I have and am doing nothing but hurting you. Have I really been so bad that you want nothing else but to escape from me? It seems that not only do you not love me, but you even have no respect for me! Sidonie I can't honestly express how dreadful I feel especially when it seems that I've made you so unhappy with my nasty and stupid ways and apparently neurotic emotions.

I've always been a lonely person, but now I feel a hundred times more lonely, I have dependants but nobody I can depend on, nobody I can turn to and say this person wants me to talk to them and wants to try and understand me, just because it's me. The person I love so very much just looks on me as a burden, a burden to be rid of as soon as possible. All my life I've been looking for someone to trust and believe in and in you I thought I had found this. You seemed to be so loyal to others, so understanding especially where people's emotions were concerned, so moved by kindness in others, so strong in your principles, in fact so different to most people, I thought that I had some of these qualities and that we could share so much together. I knew you were a better person than I, but it seems I was wrong about myself. Because if I had even some of what you have, you of all people would have recognized it. But it seems I have not.

Even now I am crying at the thought I have caused you so much pain. Please, please forgive me. I am truly sorry. Please darling if I have meant anything to you stay with me here tomorrow night. I'm begging you for those few hours.

Good night my only love.

Lenny. X.

Lenny came in and picked up the top blue sheet. On the back was written in pencil:

Dear Lenny,

We are out of milk. Could you get some from the machine, as I have no money? Thanks for the letter. See you later. Sid.

He crumpled it in his cold hand and let it lie on the floor and it was knocked into the dust under the bed by his knee as he sank down and laid his head and shoulders on the damp eiderdown and lay there until, groping in his tight pocket, his fingers penetrated the wet handkerchief and pulled out his lighter. He lit a cigarette and blundered out of the black room and could be tracked by the broken trail of a red light through the fog to the milk machine.

It was not till hours later that Lenny, lying like a

naked grub in the grey cotton cocoon, heard the door close quietly and the quick rustle and fall of clothes and felt the bed dip as she walked over him and lay next to the wall, and moving gently across the bed, felt not the sweet curve of flesh but cold denim against his trembling leg. When her breathing changed from sighs to a silent rhythm in her woollen back, he put his hand out for her zip, but when his fingertips touched metal one arm flung across the zip and the other to protect her face, which hot and breathing whisky vapour through parted lips she tossed towards him. He shone the torch on her face; she was fast asleep.

When she woke, the letter had gone and Lenny, a giant polythene bag tied round his waist for an apron, had cleared away the rubbish and was cleaning the interstices of the sink with an old sock.

He went home. She had spent the morning making lists and eaten herself into a stupor with condensed milk and slept while hours wasted in the sky, and it was six o'clock and dark when she woke and staggered off the bed lest Lenny find her there.

On Tuesday, when she came in she re-read yesterday's papers, then, exhausted by making toast, lay down on the cold bed beside the electric fire to write a letter but there was nothing to say.

Dear Chris,

Sorry I didn't reply to your letter, I lost it and couldn't remember your address till now. Are you still working at the same place? I have changed my job. How's all the family? give my love to your brother. Are you going out with anyone nice? I'm not, I could meet you any lunchtime if you like. See you soon I hope.

Love Sidonie.

She put it in an envelope and then in her pocket, where it lay. She went to sleep and when she woke, wondered for a minute if it was blood or red biro on her hand.

On Wednesday she made a list in three columns, title, artist, label, of records she wanted, made the bed.

On Thursday she put black eyebrow pencil on her lips, washed it off, cried, broke the transistor.

On Friday she made a list of 100 best tunes, 100 best films, uncompleted, 10 best painters, 10 best composers, then started a list of reasons she hated Lenny, and had it in her pocket and shoved it in her bag when it was time for love, and Lenny had gone out to get the drink, so she could bear it.

On another Monday she practised walking like John

Wayne in the mirror. Some days she could not bear Lenny to leave and sometimes when eating an egg, as the spoon pierced the albumen or pulling a comb through her hair, thoughts of Lewis would rise like split yolk and have to be pushed down or the comb rake bloody furrows through her head. A breakfast of vodka dregs and eggs, accompanied by Housewives' Choice was interrupted by Lenny breaking a teapot or kissing at her mouth; at the approach of his she shoved between her lips a cigarette, a glass, a crust, coughing was only temporary, he could crush the words of a song.

Alone in the room she felt the terrible stillness of objects, dull knives, still sheets, papers that turned only under her hand. The sun shone and set behind the dusty window, now orange against the hot box in which she sat drawing elephants backview or Donald Duck without lifting the pencil from the paper. Lenny had bought her a paintbox but when she cleaned it the first time the rag had trailed across the tin, blurring gold and turning crimson to a lake of mud. The science fiction Lenny read in the lavatory lay on the floor: 'It was the year A.D. 5000 and . . .' or subtly on the second page: ' "After all, Krog, this is A.D. 5000," he laughed.' Red biro flowers and blue vapid faces lay around on bits of paper with the word 'ambidextrous' in shaky letters.

Magazines now were mixed pleasure because the
stories made her cry.

Dear Evelyn Home,
   I am Sidonie O'Neill. What can I do?

'What on earth are you doing?'
   'Filin' my feet.'
   'Filing your feet?'
   'I'm just filin' this piece of hard skin off my foot.'
   'You'll hurt yourself.'
   'No, I don't, darlin'. Look, it's just solid skin.'
   'You think it is, but suddenly you'll gouge yourself
and then you'll know.'
   'All hard skin.'
   'Look, Lenny, could you not? I feel slightly nauseated
– not your feet, it's that terrible noise.'
   'Won't be a sec, darlin'. There, got it!' Blue shadows
fell as Lenny filed his feet and the electric fire hummed.
   'Oh God, I'm so bored.'
   'Come over here then.'
   'Not that bored.'
Lenny hygienically placed the dead skin in the rubbish
bin. Later, as he walked her to the station he was limping
and stooped to adjust his shoe.

'What's the matter?'

'You know when I was filin' my foot, I think I'm developin' a blister.'

'Buy some plaster.'

'I won't bother.'

Pam, in a scarlet tricel pleated shift, reduced to fifteen shillings and slightly long, handed her a telegram and watched while she read:

Dad injured. Please come home. Love Mother.

'I've got to go home.' She shoved it at Pam and put on her coat again.

'Her father's injured.'

'Shut up.'

'There's no need to talk to the child like that.'

Pam called 'Good Luck' from the top of the stairs.

Her father was in hospital when she got home. A note from her mother told her to meet her outside the ward. The lady next door told her he had been operated on. He had been painting a second-floor window frame and slipped and in falling had kicked the ladder, so that he landed with his legs between separate rungs and his thighs had to be freed with a hammer, the hacksaw being mislaid. His head just missed a tin of green paint, so he was spared comedy. She remembered many times she had stood in the freezing wind holding nails or searching with numb fingers for obsolete tools and non-existent clean rags.

She had thought it would not matter what one wore in a tragedy, but looking at the people waiting outside the swing doors of the ward, realized her mistake. They were all dressed up. A little girl with traces of eczema at her knees and nylon gloves frilled at the wrist jumped up and down the corridor, hanging on to arms, adjusting her hair and treading on the foot of an old man. Three women wore fur coats and all carried great bunches of irises, tulips and daffodils, scentless in the disinfected air, and knew the ranks of nurses.

She saw her mother, also out of uniform but carrying the regulation flowers, and didn't see him at first, but her mother walked straight to a bed on the left-hand row near the far end and she had to follow past the eyes on pillows and visitors already seated, their bodies familiar on the plastic and tubular chairs beside faces which did not light up at their approach. Her mother sat down and she had to stand, flicking over the pages of a newspaper that lay near the lump of feet. While her mother bent her head to find a handkerchief and a tear fell into her handbag, she told him she had got a rise at work.

Visitors and patients glanced often at the clock, but time passed very slowly. He kicked weakly at the blankets and muttered and rolled the utility head that controlled his mass-produced body in the public bed, while multiple injuries bled and writhed and bled into each other under the white chest, whose grey tufts of hair would poke through the holes of his string vest. Mrs O'Neill asked again if he was to have another operation, and he shouted:

'Ask the flaming nurse, don't ask me.'

And everyone turned and in the little silence that followed someone was sick in a bowl and the nurse, with flaming cheeks, rang the bell. He closed his eyes and the nails clenched on the grey blanket were still rimmed with Polyfilla.

When they got home she switched on the television and flaked out in a chair, and when they washed up she knew the exact position of each plate and cup. At eleven o'clock she was drinking hot chocolate when the door closed and her mother, answering the telephone, dropped the receiver on the table with a little scream and her father walked in, his shirt bulging with bandage, having discharged himself and caught a bus home. He had great shadows under his eyes and cheekbones and a bandage muffler at his throat. When his wife had helped him to bed and telephoned the hospital, they said they were sending an ambulance;

'Don't send him back,' said Sidonie, holding down the receiver. 'Can't you see – '

'See what?'

' – he doesn't want to go.'

He asked her for a glass of beer and drank a little; the froth hung yellowish on his pale mouth. She went into her room and walked round, looked out of the window, bit her hands, thought embarrassedly, 'Please don't let him die'. She stared in the mirror at the face given by him and so dissimilar, then went and listened outside her parents' room and heard two voices, so she went and lay on her bed and switched on the radio, but realizing she was waiting for a sad song, switched it off. Half an hour later she heard a cry from the bedroom, 'You can't!' and ran and opened her door, then, 'You promised me everything and you gave me nothing,' broken off with sobbing. She ran to their room and her mother, tears spurting down her wet face and saliva on her chin, beat the door with flat palms, screaming, 'Get out, get out, get out.' She pushed open the door, cutting her hand on the handle, and saw her father's head was on one side and beer was flowing in a dark brown stain on the carpet. She shut the door and didn't see him again.

The mirror in her room showed her face white with reddening eyes. She had been afraid she wouldn't be able to cry. Then she phoned her uncle to assume command and switched on the electric fire and sat down to assimilate her grief.

She went to Beacons' the two evenings later to collect a black dress and stayed the night. She woke from a dream with a piece of wire sticking through her mattress and the feeling there was something she had to do. She did not have to remember what day it was, but got out of bed to see if her stockings were dry. The windows of the room, where Joyce still slept, her open lips pushed against the pillow, were steamy and the gas fire was hot. In the defiled bathroom, garlands of paper hung round the cold geyser, and water flowed under the wheels of a red truck which squelched as if on mud and a wet heap of pyjamas in the bath showed that Royston was naked among the biscuit crumbs in the kitchen. She put a shilling in the meter and washed the soap. The dark shadows under her eyes disappeared with soap and water and were returned by the damp towel, and before the adult Beacons rose she was on the train for Penge.

Sidney O'Neill was buried two days later. His wife's family, one of whom at almost any given time could be found lying in tears on her bed, stepped from the cars checking their sorrow in bits of lace and linen and khaki. Mrs Ruby O'Neill, who had four times witnessed death; a neighbour crushed, her parents purple in a gas leakage, their Christmas dinner half-digested on the floor, her dying husband's pear-shaped head on the pillow, and her son's washed face; still believed in a benevolent God and the sanctity of life, the miracle of babies who learn to knit with their feet, but was unable to join in the hymns. At the request of the widow, 'Abide With Me' was played, which her brothers sang less heartily than at the Cup Final.

'It's your mother I feel sorry for, Sidonie,' whispered her uncle through speckled lips. 'I've a good mind to sue that hospital. Didn't they tell him he was on the bloody danger list?' A pigeon, the shot purple and green of his neck disappearing, walked with pink feet on the white granite chips. The family walked down to the church path. An aunt in motley, the thicker texture of one pale calf showing that she wore invisible support hose, her black cap bell-less but ludicrous, her bladder concealed but prominent in her mind, swung her legs into the car and said, 'Perhaps it was for the best, dear,' and quickly shut the door when she realized it wasn't.

Sidonie went to the car, where her mother hovered

with her grandmother, the driver already at the wheel, and her uncle's voice behind them:

'Didn't he know he was on the bloody danger list?'

When they got home, Sidonie made a cup of tea and washed up and had intended to go to her room:

'You're a good girl,' said her grandmother, who turned off televisions in other people's houses, as she took her empty cup. 'Turn on the television if you want, dear. He wouldn't have wanted us to be miserable.' So she had to watch the Woodentops while they wept.

After four days, Mrs O'Neill senior, decided to go home to Hull suddenly in the afternoon. A wind had risen over the gardens as she stood with dry hollyhocks clashing above her head in the white sky as at the threat of rain she took down her washing and hurried into the house to pack.

When both her dresses were too dirty to wear any longer, and she was tired of leaving the receiver off the hook or promising Lenny over the phone to return soon, Sidonie had to think about going back to Beacons.

'I don't know what I'll do here by myself,' moaned her mother. 'I suppose I could ask Aunt Doris to move in.'

'You hate her.'

'I know.'

'I'll come and live here.' Sidonie said what she was intended to say and realized it was what she wanted, and came and went in the desolated but comfortable house, singing under her breath, until she remembered she would have to face the Beacons and Joyce.

Joyce was easy; she met her for lunch.

'I sort of thought you might, so I looked at the notice board, but they mostly wanted a third Kiwi, but I heard that a friend from work's flat mate's going to Canada. So I'll probably move in with her. I can't wait to get away from the Beacons. They've been even worse since you went away, Sid; Lenny hasn't been working, he just sits glaring at Pam all evening, and the television's broken. Oh yes, did I tell you they had a party the other night and Pam threw herself off the balcony?'

'What?'

'Yes, but there was a man underneath in the street and he caught her and she just came upstairs again. Lenny didn't even notice.'

On the way home she met Lewis.

'Sorry about your Dad.'

'So am I.'

'I've seen you a couple of times out with the dog. I wanted to speak to you. I'm off work with flu.'

'You should have.' They walked to her gate and

stood against the wet privet while the green iron fence dripped.

'I don't suppose you'll want to, but would you like to come out with me one evening, on a friendly basis of course?'

'When for instance?'

'Tomorrow.'

'All right. I'll have to see what my mother's doing.'

At ten to four on a wild Wednesday Sidonie was in position with a small suitcase and a bag behind a pillar at the wrong end of the road, but pressed herself in horror into a wet hedge as a pram, pushed by a running woman, lurched up the wet pavement towards her, but as it approached, knees buckled and teeth jutted and the dark imposter in the pram was more beautiful than a Beacon. Then another pram bumped down the steps and turned in the opposite direction, a little girl hanging on the handle; the wheel ran over her foot and she was lifted kicking on to the pram and her screams were heard until they turned the corner.

Sidonie ran down the road and quietly fitted her key into the lock; she left the front door open and was half-way up stairs when she was frozen in the creaking dust by voices. They grew fainter, as if from behind a closed door, and Sidonie, her hand squeaking up the bannister, reached the bathroom, where bubbling with steam and water, Lenny's voice sang through the frosted glass. The kitchen door was closed on shouts and music. Pam must just be shopping, which meant less time. Two beer cans had rolled a sticky trail through the dust behind her old door; she tried to lock it but the latch was broken, Joyce's bed unmade. What noise she made, ripping dresses from hangers and tearing apart the embrace of woollen arms from the heap on the floor, the sigh of nylon and the whine of a recalcitrant drawer, was drowned by Beacon's watery bass. As she started shoving books into the other bag, the door opened and a little figure, face flushed, chest heaving under a slipping striped rug stood in the doorway and shouted, 'I not tiger!'

'Of course you're a tiger, you little fool.'

He turned and ran out. She shut the door and heard the bathroom door open.

'Daddy, I not a little fool.'

'Of course you are, dear,'

She had got most of her clothes into the case and swept lipstick stubs and solidified nail varnish on top of her books and emptied in half the record rank. She left a little pile of dead shoes and stockings, to be a post-humous humiliation.

When she was on the third stair, the pram brake slammed on and a carrier bag was bumped up the steps. She ran down the stairs and pushed her bag into Pam's soft doubled stomach, her flying hair caught on Sidonie's button and her head was jerked round, red mouth shrieking like a gargoyle. Sidonie kicked the front door and ran down the steps into the street as Lenny, knocking Pam against the wall and sending the carrier bag flying in a shower of tins, grabbed glass and wood as the door slammed in his face. She reached Earls Court Road as a taxi slowed down for the lights, and Pam's voice screamed after her running husband:

'Let her go, Lenny!'
and waving her bags at it, fled into the taxi as the lights turned to green, and Lenny grimaced through the blue glass; and sat a hank of brown hair blowing from her button in the wind from the open window.

'Pal for my pal, Chum for my chum' – she was forking the meat into a plate marked Dog – 'Your fresh sweet kiss thrills me so' – and put it down beside the water-bowl, where an insomniac Jacky had left shreds of greaseless margarine paper. He lay with his head on his front paws, brown eyes staring, and gave long whistling sighs. When she looked at him he closed his eyes. When she called him, 'Jacky, come and get your dinner', he danced to the tasteless food, leaving an old glove soggy in his basket. She, who had since he was a puppy, considered him just a furry appendage attached to her father by a light chain lead, was grateful for the way his soft mouth deigned to accept from her fingers Winalot and selected meats from the supermarket, standing white and silver in a shaft of light, allowing himself to be dependent on her. So she began to vary his diet, adding cheese for protein and chopped butcher's meat, and big bones for teeth, ignoring splintering little ones that might pierce the red throat that yawned all evening and bayed wide awake when she took down his lead for a late walk.

As she took Jacky to the park, she learned how an animal, by existing, having fur and faculties can glorify the life of a human being. When she cried, when the great black retriever lifted him by his gold and silver neck and dashed him to the path, sending him spinning with red fang marks frothing in his fur, it was because in his maturity the warrior had become a pacifist, even a conscientious objector. She picked him up at the side of the path and would have carried him, but he insisted on walking home. He lapped a little water with his eyes laid back and lay behind a chair to clean his fur, not wanting comfort.

The wounds were slight and soon healed. He was a pleasure to take out, leaping through long lakes left by rain in the grass, drowning the inverted trees and sky. In the dark days at Beacons, she had dreamed of lying on hot Greek rocks while sun and wine and grapes healed mind and body, but she was finding salvation in wet London parks. She noticed how quickly dead worms assimilate the colour of the earth or pavement; clitellum, segments dry to dust or glitter with frost.

The fifth time she met Lewis he asked her to marry him and she said yes, and was happy, despite guilt at thinking there's always divorce. Alone with Lewis, or with friends in noisy public bars or saloons with pools of light and pale pools of gin, she never asked for whisky or gin and tonic, because with the sip, the smell, the slice of lemon, came the pain of Pam and Earls Court nights, but asked for, and the clean-shaven faces, or bearded but decent, ordered and set down in front of her, unseasonable light and lime or lager and lime in tall innocuous glasses, or half of bitter in its solid glass whose opaque facets did not reflect.

One afternoon, Sidonie came in from posting an application for a job, her hair soaked by a sudden storm.

'Better give that hair a good rub.'

Beacon was seated at her mother's table, eating cake. She stood dripping, as he violated the cup.

'Don't look so surprised, dear – I'm not a ghost. See, solid flesh.'

Mrs O'Neill laughed; the doctor had prescribed sleeping pills.

'Have a cup of tea, dear.'

She poured one, and the saucer slipped and Lenny said, 'Same clumsy old Sid,' and Mrs O'Neill looked surprised. He offered cigarettes and to wash up.

'Pam and the kids have been wondering why you haven't been to see them.'

'Oh.'

'You could go over any afternoon,' said Mrs O'Neill.

'Why are you down here?'

'I had to see a bloke about a car.' He had been driven down, and when he left, asked Mrs O'Neill the way to the station and she suggested Sidonie should go with him.

'I've got a job. I'll be sending you the arrears of rent gradually. You can tell Pam.'

'Don't be ridiculous, dear. By the way, I'm very hurt by the way you left.'

'How's Pam?'

'Still having it off with old Dickey.'

'Dickey!'

'Of course, you didn't know, did you, dear. I'm sorry, perhaps I shouldn't have told you.'

'I don't care. There's the station.'

Lenny bought a ticket.

'Pam doesn't know I've seen you today.'

'Are she and Dickey all in love?'

'According to Pam, he's got it bad.'

'Needless to say she hasn't.'

'When can I see you?'

'Never.'

'Darlin'.'

'Let go of my arm.'

'I'll be here at ten o'clock on Wednesday.'

'Here's your train.'

'I'll be waitin' here at ten on Wednesday.'

'You'll have a long wait.'

He grabbed her hands and nuzzled his wet head at her as the train stopped. 'I've nothing now you've gone, give me this one last thing.'

'Oh, all right. Get in, for Christ's sake.'

'I don't care' and caring were synonymous when she woke suddenly at the bitter hour of four and thought of Pam still dancing.

She seldom thought of the high house where the

Beacons ate their lunch at four, while insane tradesmen conspired below.

Beacon came, beating the cold with his open coat.

'I dreamed about you last night again.'

'Oh.'

He put his feet on the dusty red seat opposite as the train left.

'We were on a lonely beach together. It was night time. You were crying and I comforted you.'

'You probably made me cry in the first place.'

He squeezed her hand all the way on the train and on the Underground to Leicester Square. He had to pick up some money from his office and she waited on adjacent steps till he came out, putting his wallet in his pocket. The finger of his leather gloves, a relic of the drunken and dismal Christmas, was rough and she saw that Pam had cobbled it where he had chewed.

'This is where the fun begins,' said Beacon, holding open the frosted door of an empty pub. When they came out, the cold was less severe, Beacon his most charming. A cloud was blown away, light streamed on Beacon's face, he stopped with outstretched arms. At that moment he had no need of hair.

Lenny came back from the bar and went down to the gents. When he returned, a man was leaning over

Sidonie; he had Slav cheek-bones and his breath smelled of crisps –

'Let's get out of here.'

She didn't know who said it.

'Drinking bloody shorts!' said Lenny, after he had accepted a drink and gone. As the pub emptied, he bought half a bottle of whisky. They walked across Bond Street and were somewhere in its environs when Lenny insisted they eat. Cream cheese and asparagus sandwiches and coffee were served by a freckled waitress, who seemed to smile too much.

'Do we look drunk?' said Lenny, pouring sugar into the handle of his spoon.

In the street, Sidonie went down some steps and Lenny followed into a big room with two billiard tables and chairs stacked round the wall. She tore the cloth with a cue and dropped it with a crash to the floor, and they ran behind a thick curtain. No one came.

'Stop it, Lenny.'

'You like it.'

He passed her the bottle. They had been sitting on a bench, but were now on the floor.

'What do you think this place is?'

'Some kind of Services club. There's a coat of arms on the door.'

'You know, Lenny, sometimes I quite like you, but I suppose it's only the drink.'

'Darlin'!'

'All right, it isn't. Where is it? Thank you. You know, I used to think, although of course one would prefer romantic ideas, that the perfect place and state of mind to be in, was at a party, alien in unknown bathrooms; you forget the past and you're disorientated from the present, there's just these white tiles and maybe a window, and when you go upstairs it's all dancing and drinking.'

'I thought you couldn't dance.'

'I could till I met you.'

'Sometimes you make me feel that all I've done is hurt you.'

He held the bottle to her lips until she coughed and then to his.

'Are you asleep?'

'No, thinking.'

'What about, darlin'?'

'Nothing.'

'You always keep your thoughts from me. Am I too stupid or uneducated to understand them?'

'Of course not, stupid. Lenny, don't.'

'Yes, darlin'.'

'Is there any left?'

He gave her the bottle.

'Don't stop me, darlin'.'

'Yes. I must. You don't understand.'

'Tell me and I'll try.'

'I can't – oh – I can't, it's too stupid.'

She whispered into his ear, inclined like a dried apricot. 'I've got a horrible feeling my father's watching me.'

He took her hand. 'Darlin', he can't see you.'

She knew he could, but Lenny was moving in towards her mouth.

Breaking loose from Lenny's kiss she finished the bottle.

'I wonder where those steps lead to?'

They led into a cloakroom. While Beacon was in a cubicle, she washed her face and threw a handful of cold water over his door. He screamed and burst out and turned on all the taps, knocking a glass from a rack, and sheets of water shot across the floor and the air was shattered with screams. Beacon was bleeding on the face; the water had concealed a piece of glass.

'Oh darlin', my darlin',' he stretched out his arms and cracked his forehead on her reflection in the glass. A man came in and gazing at the flooded floor, said to Sidonie:

'What the hell are you doing here?'

Water thundered into empty basins.

'I don't know.'

She waited for Lenny in the doorway and they walked stiffly, with spattered coats, into the freezing air.

'I sorted that bastard out.'

'How?'

'When he turned round, I sneaked back to the wash basin and let him have a glassful right in the face.'

'Where are we?'

'Oh my God,' said Lenny, and rushing to the gutter, was sick over the boot of a reversing Jaguar whose driver, saluting a passing taxi, drove elegantly away.

'I don't know what's the matter with me. Some of that beer must have been off.'

The sky was pink and four o'clock showed on an enamelled clock. Lenny stood in front of a ground floor mirror in a shop, his ears crumpled beneath a green straw hat. He crammed his head into a tartan jockey cap.

'Can I help you?'

'No, thank you.'

A senior saleslady approached, so Sidonie led him to another floor.

'I want an evening dress for my daughter,' she said, indicating Lenny, who had already swept an armful of dresses from the racks. The assistant pulled back the edge of the velvet fitting-room curtain and her face froze in the mirror at Lenny, arms flailing from a grey vest, underpants open, bald head sticking through a silver-satin arm-hole hopping on one foot, his heavy shoe caught in the net under-skirt. When the assistant came back with the manageress, Sidonie placed a pile of dresses, all on their hangers, in her arms.

'I don't think any of these are quite suitable, thank you,' and holding Lenny's hand tightly, his wedding ring grinding his finger, led him past a little crowd of women, down the stairs and into the street and to a coffee bar. Something, perhaps only their faces in the mirror, was familiar, but when the menu was brought by a smiling freckled waitress, Sidonie realized they were in the same place as before and rushed out leaving a plastic menu flapping in Lenny's hand. Then a wet wind blew round the corner and the sky darkened; as great drops of rain fell they huddled in a doorway and the door opened suddenly under Lenny's weight and he fell backwards into the pink light. Behind him were carpeted stairs. They went up, past a pink hairdressing salon on the first floor and came to a little empty office with the light on. Lenny sat down, his feet on the desk.

'Take a letter, Miss O'Neill.'

'Certainly not.' He was like a child running out to the teacher's desk to imitate her when she left the room.

'Take this.' She handed him a cut-glass decanter. He took it by the stopper and it crashed on to his foot, spraying the front of his trousers with whisky. He limped out after her.

'Remember that time we didn't pay our bill in that restaurant and you forgot your briefcase and had to go back for it and the manager thanked you for coming back?'

'What of it?'

'Nothing.'

At the top of the building, stairs changed to rungs and Sidonie stuck her head through a door into a gust of rain and darkness. Below, the lights of cars were jammed together and people hurried with umbrellas and rushed from lighted doorways to hail engaged taxis. Beacon stood beside her on the roof, his open mouth catching rain like a pelican's beak. Then at the sound of steps and voices beaks snapped shut and they ran downstairs past a uniformed man, who grabbed at them and shouted, and down the road.

They sat in a cinema and came out at nine half blinded into the lights and rain and took a taxi to a club in Earls

Court, where a friend of Sidonie's used to be a croupier. She asked for him at the door and he came out, rubies flashing at the cuffs of a crumpled pink shirt. He was just going to play and sat down at the green table. Lenny and Sidonie went into another room, where two people danced to the jukebox on the parquet floor. A woman, arms stretched stiffly from the straps of a black dress, sat with her head on the bar, her handbag round her ankle and a black patent shoe in her hand, her face, corroded like a lemon in the single yellow light above, stared from a mirror.

'Pam's pregnant,' said Lenny shuffling his little feet to the music.

'Oh no!'

'Oh yes,' he sang.

She sat on a stool at the bar.

'Are you pleased?'

'I'd kick her in the stomach if I thought it would do any good.'

Sidonie remembered what she had to do.

'How's Pam feel?'

'Sick.'

'About the baby.'

'I think the cow did it on purpose.'

'Why?'

'To keep me. She thinks she's got me now and she means to keep me.'

'And hasn't she?'

'You've got me, darlin' – body and soul.'

'You haven't got one.'

'What do you mean I haven't got a soul?'

'Body.'

She saw he was about to cry and excused herself. A silk and mohair jacket hung on the door of the little bathroom. There was only a membership card in the pockets, but in the blue silk lining was a long narrow pocket. She put in her fingers and drew out a little silver pistol, no longer than her hand. She placed it in her mouth and then in her pocket. When she got back to the bar the barman slopped whisky over warm ice in her glass and Lenny handed him his last pound note.

Lenny fought his flapping coat in the dark and dragged Sidonie's hand through the rain to his pocket and they walked against the wind in the direction of Notting Hill. Three squares of light shone from their old windows; a piece of cardboard had replaced the pane and music was blown towards them and away as they stood looking up, rain beating on Lenny's head. He put his arm round her shoulder and she saw his eyes glitter in his wet face as he led her away.

'I'm so cold.'

He started to take off his coat, she refused it. The wailing wind of two o'clock drove them to the gate of a house which stood apart from its empty neighbours in a garden; and a long glass canopy led to the door. Heaps of bricks and burnt wood showed the house was partly demolished. Sidonie felt afraid, as if it was Lenny's frozen hand the gun burned. His torch flickered over black wetness and bricks to the door leaning upside down against a hanging beam. He went in and she followed, out of the rain into wind blowing through broken glass. Lenny came towards her, his mouth a pit above the torch.

'No, Lenny, no.' She backed against a wall, then remembered it was she who had the gun and took it from her pocket and pointed it in his face.

'O.K., Beacon. Start walking backwards.'

'Where did you get that thing?'

She pulled the trigger and a window shattered.

'Get walking, Beacon.'

He slipped and cracked the back of his head on a marble mantelpiece on the floor. She poked him with her foot; he leaped up, snatching at the gun, and she turned and ran upstairs and across to where Beacon's torch, waving through a great gap in the floor lit a jagged window. She pushed up the frame and climbed out on to a broad window-sill and crawled along wet stone until she was lying across the iron spine of the glass canopy. Beacon's feet rushed into the room behind her and another and thudded down the splintering stairs and into the garden. Her hand knocked an iron screw that fell to the concrete at his feet. Lenny shone his torch on a black shape through the glass.

'Sidonie?'

The shape moved and concrete shattered at his feet. He began to run down under the canopy his arms round his head, the path bursting in his face and consecutive panes shattering on him as he ran from side to side, then as he looked up, a lump of iron smashed into his forehead and he fell. Sidonie crawled backwards down the canopy and raised the window, which had fallen, glass making a bracelet of blood round each wrist. A lighter cloud lit the rusty iron frill which she had torn off with her hand and thrown, lying beside the fragments and filaments of the torch, Lenny lay face downward, groaning.

'Darlin', it bounced off my head.'

She gave him a handkerchief to wipe the black blood from his eyes.

'You've only got abrasions. Get up or I'll shoot.'

She pointed the empty gun as he lurched to his feet and took his arm and dragged him by the wet sleeve towards Earls Court. In Warwick Road he suddenly reeled over and beer and whisky poured from his mouth. She sank to the pavement beside him, her hair blown across his face. It started to rain again as she heard heavy feet coming round the corner, and she ran down a side street and into a church. The shallow water darkened in the font as she washed her hands.

She saw him once more, three months later, striding purposefully in through the exit of the Premier Supermarket.

Afterword

Rereading something you wrote a quarter of a century ago is a bit like studying the photograph on its original dust jacket and then looking in the mirror. You suppose that it was you who wrote it just as you must assume that the person in the glass is, more or less, the person in the picture, but the intervening twenty five-years bring a dimension of disbelief.

I can remember writing in Kensington library among earnest-looking overseas students, and in Holborn library, which figures in the narrative, but that is as far as my memory of what is called the creative process goes. I was about nineteen and had been living in Earls Court for about two years. Memories of my first night there are stronger: the realization that there was no going back from grubby candlewick bedspreads, suitcases on the tops of wardrobes, slot-meters for the old-style gas, which one of our fellow residents was able to feed with enough pennies to kill himself, and bathrooms shared with at least twenty other people, was tempered by the assurance of the housekeeper that Earls Court was one of the most notorious districts of London. When a friend had suggested that we share a room there I, unfamiliar with the area, had imagined from its sedate name that Earls Court would be rather like Bournemouth or Hove. Then, before the sixties had got into their swing, it was known as Kangaroo Valley: Australians, New Zealanders, white South Africans and Rhodesians had colonized the Earls Court road, Cromwell, West Cromwell, all the roads of big houses in which we had rooms. If, as we used to write as children, this book should chance to roam, as far as Zimbabwe or wherever she is now, I'd like to say hello to my old friend of those days, which were much more fun than those portrayed in it.

As to the book, there is nothing I could alter now if I wished to do so. There are, inevitably, parts of it which I can see could have been handled more skilfully, sentences which glare at me from the page. I could advize Sidonie on how to deal with certain situations and relationships, how not to fall victim to her predators, and I might have less sympathy with her passivity and more for Pam's domestic circumstances and situation; but as people and events are, except on one occasion, seen exclusively through Sidonie's eyes, such hindsights and observations are irrelevant. One thing in particular that strikes me is how small a part, despite its title, music plays in the story; in fact there was music, Motown and early Beatles, everywhere and not just upstairs.

Shena Mackay, London, 1988